Washed Up

···

Valerie Grezman

Contents

Undertow

R iley

Undertow. Noun. [uhn-der-toh]. Any strong current below the surface of a body of water, moving in a direction different from that of the surface current.

Failure.

That's the word my dad used to describe me when I told him the news over the phone two weeks ago.

"You're a failure, Riley Olson. What ever possessed you to drop out of Cornell? Do you know how much that costs us a semester?"

This was followed by a detailed breakdown of the cost of my college tuition down to the penny. I mean, I guess I deserved the dressing down he gave me. I did drop out of college after my sophomore year, and it was really expensive.

I press my flip-flopped heel harder against the gas pedal and speed down the highway, my tiny Honda Fit rattling on the pothole-covered road. So it's my own fault I'm in this mess. Is that supposed to make me feel better? Because it doesn't. Not one freaking bit.

Wind races through my car as I accelerate--60, 65, 70, 75--until the sea soaked air sends my tawny locks flying in every direction. I glance in my rearview mirror, and when I don't see any cops, I accelerate to 80 miles per hour, speeding by an Oldsmobile with an owner that matches its name.

You know what I wanted to tell Colonel Eugene Olson when he spewed his judgmental crap at me? I wanted to tell him that it takes one to know one. He may not have failed in his career--he's a Colonel in the Army who has hopes of making Brigadier General in the next few years-but he sure was a failure of a father.

I've moved 17 times in my life, 18 after my car and I make it to our destination, and most of those times were because of my dad and his job. While most of Dad's coworkers refused promotions because they didn't want to uproot their families and move to a new state or even country, my dad always took the jobs, and my mom and I were dragged along for the ride. When I finally graduated from high school while we lived in Camp Atterbury, Indiana, I immediately enrolled at Cornell University. I never planned on going back to my life as an Army brat.

The first semester of college was a blast; I loved having a roommate and a little family on my floor. I wasn't used to having friends since we'd never stayed in one place for very long, so I treasured the new-found intimacy with my floormates. But by the second semester, my roommate and I started to fight about stupid stuff: missing socks, stolen snacks, loud music, dirty dishes. By the end of year one, I was fed up with her, so I signed up for study abroad for the fall. I lived in Italy for the semester and loved the sightseeing and culture. I enjoyed traveling through parts of Europe I had never been before and I even picked up a little Italian. Mi chiamo Riley! Impressive, right?

Spring semester, I got a new roommate and started to take some classes in my major, Business Administration. I hated them. I've never been great with organization or money or anything like that, but Dad said a Business degree would get me a good job after graduation, so I listened to him, but I ended up hating the classes. They didn't interest me, and I didn't do well at them. When I started to get B's instead of the A's I was used to, I decided I was done. I knew I couldn't change my major without Dad threatening to stop paying my tuition, so my decision was made. By the end of my sophomore year, I hated everything about college, and since I'm 20 now, my life is in my own hands. I decided to drop out.

I don't regret dropping out of college, but I do regret where it led me: Long Beach Island, New Jersey. Most people would be thrilled about spending their summer at the beach, but I'm not. More specifically, I'm not thrilled about spending twelve weeks living with people I've never met and working in a pizza shop serving over-enthusiastic tourists.

The wind whipping my hair into my face grows saltier and I breathe in the smell. This summer wouldn't be so bad if I could spend it on the beach. I love the outdoors. In every place I've ever lived, I always find someplace outdoors by myself that makes it all bearable. After move number six, I gave up on trying to make lasting friendships. Finding a place to be alone with my thoughts has pretty much been my only solace. Even at Cornell and in Italy, I always found a place where I could be alone with nature.

The highway winds over a hill and I slow down when I see the bay, a huge bridge covering the distance between the mainland and the long, slender island. My new home. I almost laugh out loud. The word "home" has lost all meaning to me. I've had seventeen homes, but none of them felt like what a home should feel like. Or at least what I assume a home should feel like. In the movies, a home is always filled with love, laughter, and support. It's steady and constant, a place to run to when things are hard. I guess the outdoors have been my only home, but I imagine the beach will be too busy to be much of a refuge for me this summer.

I cross the bridge, and my heart starts to pound. I'm not sure why I'm nervous. This is my 18th move; I should be used to the process by now. Unpack your meager possessions. Find a grocery store, a gas station, a convenience store. Don't get attached to anyone. This time is different, however. Before, I was always with my parents so I could hide behind them and then scuttle off to my room when anyone tried to talk to me. This time, however, I have to meet Mr. and Mrs. Jennings and thank them profusely for agreeing to take my parents' prodigal daughter under their wing for the summer. This time, I'm on my own.

I think Mom sent me here because she felt bad for me and she knew better than to try to change Dad's mind. Mom told me that her and my dad used to spend their summers on this island all through college, working part time jobs and living in a crappy mainland apartment. They stayed on the beach any time they weren't working, rode bikes up and down the island, and made friends with all of the people who lived there year round like the Jennings. Since my parents are stationed in the U.A.E. right now, they couldn't fly me over to join them so they sent me here as an apology.

I should be grateful. I'm using this summer to figure out what to do with my life. By the end of the summer, I'll have my feet back under me. I'll find a full-time job myself doing something that I love--still have to figure out what that is--and I won't have to rely on my parents' restrictive generosity any longer. I have twelve weeks--93 days, to be exact--to figure out just what that looks like. For now, I'm caught in the undertow, but by the end of this summer, I'll be riding the waves like a pro.

Line Up

R^{oss}
Line up. Noun. [lahyn uhp]. The place just outside the breaking waves where surfers wait for their waves.

I lean my head against the wooden back of the lifeguard chair, my eyes lazily scanning the two kids playing in the sand at the edge of the waves. Sun beats down on my face, deepening my already golden brown complexion, and wind tickles the soft cotton of my t-shirt.

Summer. It officially starts tomorrow, bringing the crowds of Mainlanders with their garish beach umbrellas, screaming toddlers, and inability to doggy paddle in the whitecaps. As a year-round islander, I have mixed feelings about the dawn of summer. On one hand, summer brings a huge boost in income to my dad's part-time bike rental business, and I get paid for longer hours as a lifeguard during the prime months for beach going. On the other hand, my peaceful beach will be packed with half-naked tourists instead of wild horses. I'll look out to the ocean and see drowning teenagers instead of pods of dolphins.

Financially, summer's great. I don't have to drive to the mainland every day to work in the Office Max warehouse, loading boxes in the sweltering heat. I get to spend my days in this chair with my rescue tube beside me and my lifeguard whistle around my neck. Sure, I'll have to dive into the freezing waves to rescue a few idiots, but it's a small price to pay for a summer spent on the beach.

After working as a lifeguard for eleven summers, however, I itch for something more. I love the beach and the ocean and my island, but there's more to the world than the sound of the lapping waves and the feel of sand between my toes. I'm not sure what more, but I know there has to be something beyond life tied to one miniscule strip of land next to the Atlantic coast.

I watch as one of the kids passes the black and white checkered flag marking the edge of the swim zone and I lift the whistle to my lips and motion him back into the safe area.

"Still strict as ever, Rossy."

I look down from my chair to find Javier and Earnest, two of the other summer lifeguards I've known for years.

"It's about time you Mainlanders got here," I say, jumping from the chair into the soft sand ten feet below me.

I shake hands with Javier, a spunky Mexican American kid who talks too much, and slap Earnest on the back, disturbing his perfectly combed hair and pressed dress shirt. Javier and Earnest are summer lifeguards, living here for June, July, and August and then returning to their normal Mainland lives.

"How's Dartmouth, Ernie?" I ask, eying the dark haired kid with the serious expression.

"Still in New Hampshire," he responds with a half quirked smile.

Javier slaps him on the back. "Hilarious, Ernie. Real funny. How's our island, Ross? Ready for us?"

"After three years ago?" I joke, remembering the illegal fireworks we set off on the 4th of July.

That almost landed us in jail, but luckily, Earnest runs track, Javier plays soccer, and I run on the beach every morning. We were fast enough to leave our inexperienced Long Beach law enforcement in our dust. Even though Bob Warner and the other local cops know we were the culprits, they couldn't pin anything on us and let it slide.

Still, I'm 24 now, too old for the carefree summer antics of yore. The novelty of spending the summer on the beach wore off years ago, but I don't have any other choices. Instead of enjoying it like I should, I feel stuck here in a Groundhog's Day loop of the same summer, year after year after year.

I glance back at the beach and blow my whistle when I see a gang of surfers getting too close to the surf zone like I've done a thousand times. I tamp down my discontentment and turn to Javier and Earnest.

"I'm still on duty, guys. A good lifeguard never sleeps."

"Nah, he only naps when no one's looking," Javier says, winking. He scales the chair beside me and we share the wooden bench made for two.

Earnest remains standing below us, rolling his eyes at Javier and checking his phone.

"What's the matter, Ernie? Waiting for Lucy to text you back?" Javier teases, recalling Earnest's summer girlfriend of the last three years, Lucy Covington, an islander like me.

"Screw off, Jav," Earnest responds, but the red on the tips of his ears tells us Javier was right.

We both laugh and I ask, "When did you guys get here?"

"Just a few minutes ago. Zack told us you were down here so we thought we'd stop by and say hello," Earnest answers.

"Oh, dang," I say. "So you really are waiting to see Lucy."

Javier cracks up beside me, slapping his knee and sending peals of laughter across the water. He disturbs a flock of seagulls and sends them flying further down the beach. Earnest sighs and rolls his eyes at both of us.

"You knuckleheads might not be aware, but some people actually want to see each other after months apart."

Earnest's name has always matched his personality. While Javier is all jokes and wild pranks, Earnest is serious, forthright, and sincere. I lie somewhere in between them on the spectrum, laid back enough to avoid being the brunt of all the jokes, but not as untamed as Javier.

"Months?" Javier asks, "You mean you've seen your little Lucy Liu since last summer?"

"She visited me a few months ago," Earnest answers, rocking back and forth in the sand.

I smile to myself as Javier interrogates him, trying to unearth the juicy details. It doesn't surprise me that Earnest and Lucy have gotten more serious; the tenor of their relationship changed last summer, becoming something that lasts beyond the summer months. It's been so long since I've actually dated that I forget what anything beyond meaningless flings and casual flirtations feels like. Maybe I'm jealous of what Earnest and Lucy have, that it lasts beyond the fleeting heat of summer.

"Go see your girlfriend," I finally say.

"Yeah, she's a lot prettier to look at than this ogre," Javier says, elbowing me in the ribs and cackling.

Earnest doesn't hesitate to jog off the beach to find her, leaving me with Javier.

"Speaking of girlfriends, Monica's back," he says in a singsong voice.

I cringe, recalling mistakes of years gone by. Monica Chanel was a summer lifeguard from two years ago who looked way too hot in her lifeguard swimsuit. So hot, in fact, that I convinced myself I couldn't resist her. One three week fling later, I realized she also knew she was too hot to resist and I wasn't the only lifeguard who had caught her interest.

"Great. I'll have to ask Zack to keep us off the same beach." I turn to Javier, watching the sunlight play in the dark chestnut of his eyes as he gazes out over the waves. "How about you, Jav? What's new?"

"Eh, nothing," he answers, scratching his shoulder. "I've been good."

His words ring hollow. "Really? Any news on your dad?"

A few years ago, Javier's dad was arrested for illegal immigration. His family lives in a poorer part of Philly and five or so years ago, their house burnt down and all of their immigration papers went up in flames. His dad had no green card to show, so they deported him back to Mexico, leaving Javier, his American-born mother, and his six siblings behind.

"No." Javier's jaw tenses. "Mom's thinking about taking the younger kids and moving back to Mexico. I don't make enough to take care of all of us and Dad's in Mexico, so..."

I don't say anything but I look away. I'm not a stranger to having to take care of a family. I've been taking care of Dad and my three younger siblings for years. Usually I like being able to help my family, but sometimes I feel like they shackle me to the island, keeping me from exploring the vast world outside of Long Beach.

Sometimes I feel like I'm just waiting for a wave to sweep me off my feet instead of riding the waves myself.

Surf's Up

Riley

Surf's Up. Noun. [surfs uhp]. The conditions of the waves and weather are favorable for surfing.

The sign says, "Welcome to Long Beach Island" and I realize I'm probably the first person to ever set foot on this island who isn't thrilled to be here, but I'd much rather be somewhere I want to be. Hiking through Yosemite, eating brunch in Paris...heck, I'd rather be eating Cheetos in my underwear in a run-down motel in the middle of Kansas than be moving to this random island to live with people I've never met.

"Positivity, Riley," I can hear my mom squawking at me while hiding behind her rose gold iPhone and perfectly manicured nails.

Positivity doesn't do squat. I prefer realism--I don't want to be here, but there's nothing I can do about it. At some point, I'm going to have to accept that I'm stranded here for the summer, but today is not that day. Cue Lord of the Rings fight music.

This summer, I'm living with the Covingtons. They sound like they should be descendants of old British royalty, but apparently they run a pizza shop, so I'm not quite sure what to expect. After I dropped out, I pleaded with Mom and Dad to let me go with them to Dubai, but they refused, saying something about "consequences." I understand consequences; my dad's in the freaking Army. A consequence is being forced to jog three miles for forgetting to rinse off your dinner plate. But I'm 20. Yes, I made a mistake. Yes, I dropped out of college. But that shouldn't be the end. I should be able to choose my own path, but I guess it would help if I knew where that path led. The poor Covingtons, stuck with me for the summer.

I can just hear Mom now. "Riley's a little..." Insert awkward laugh. "Troubled. I think spending some time with you this summer will give her a great opportunity. Maybe she can learn a little from your daughter."

With the way my mom talks about me, you would think I was a meth dealer who's pregnant with twins and has 33 piercings, but no. I'm just a girl who doesn't know where she belongs. I thought maybe I belonged at college, or maybe in Italy, but no. No place, no person, seems right for me. So here I am. Long Beach freaking Island.

I guess I just keep expecting them to let me make mistakes. It's only human, right? Wrong. Not in my family. We don't make mistakes because, as my dad reminds me time after time, "Mistakes cost lives in the Army, Riley." With no room for error, of course I'm going to fall short of their standards. I just didn't expect to get exiled as punishment for my failure.

I turn off of the bridge onto the main stretch that goes down the narrow island. From the first red light, I can already see the crest of the beach to my left and the bay to my right. I slow down in the traffic that's already congested even though summer doesn't start until tomorrow. A family of five, the three kids all under eight, traipse across the street in front of me in bright swimsuits, hauling chairs, a beach umbrella, and a cooler behind them. They throw back their heads and laugh, reminiscent of a bad TV ad for Ocean City.

I double check my phone for the location of the Covingtons' house and take in the sights as I inch through the traffic. A thousand little shops line the street, each with overpriced t-shirts, souvenirs, or food. The smell of saltwater mixed with fried fish lingers in the air and I roll the windows down. Okay, positivity. I've always loved the smell of the ocean air. In all the beaches and seas I've visited across the world, there's nothing like the smell of the Atlantic Ocean.

The moment is ruined when a big splat of seagull poop lands in the middle of my windshield. Great. I run my windshield wipers but the crap just smears all the way across. I sigh and run a hand through my hair which is already starting to frizz in the humid air. This is really not my day. Or month. Or year.

At the next stop light, I take a right and spot the place where I'm going: A Pizza the Action. That's legitimately its name. I groan at the terrible pun and pull into an empty parking spot in the back of the lot. Despite the name, the place is packed with customers and I stand outside for a moment and watch the commotion through the front window. An Asian girl works furiously behind the counter, spewing out pizza boxes left and right. The customers inhale their food and leave with smiles on their faces and friendly waves to the girl at the counter.

I sigh and return to my car, grabbing my duffel bag and suitcase with the majority of my earthly possessions. After 17 moves, I've learned that material goods are trivial and I don't need much to survive. Survive. That's been my entire life. Have I ever really lived?

I brush aside the philosophical quandary and haul my stuff to the front door of the pizza shop. When the door dings as I walk in, the crowd quiets and stares at the girl with her life packed in a suitcase dragging behind her. I stall in the door and look around with bug eyes. I don't even know what the Covingtons look like; how am I going to even introduce myself? "Hi, I'm the Olsons' prodigal daughter come for rehab." Somehow, I doubt that would go over well.

The girl from behind the counter wipes her greasy palms on her apron and bounces toward me, hand outstretched. "Hi! You must be Riley Olson."

I almost check if I'm wearing a nametag. "Uh, yeah. I am."

"Great!" She offers a huge smile. "I'm Lucy. I'm so excited you're here! This is going to be a great summer."

I have a bad feeling she was a cheerleader in high school. "Oh, Lucy Covington? Hi."

"That's me! Here, let's go meet my parents, and I can show you where we'll be living."

She takes my suitcase out of my hand and heads behind the counter. The customers grumble as I follow her behind the counter into the kitchen. A sweaty teenager and two adults run frantically back and forth, hand tossing pizza dough, sprinkling pepperoni, pulling hot pizzas from the ovens. Despite the chaos, when Lucy yells, both adults stop and turn to us.

Mr. and Mrs. Covington are precious, pudgy little people. They greet me with wide smiles on their round, flour-dusted faces. When they see me, they scream in unison and rush towards me, pulling me into overly intimate hugs that smell like tomato sauce.

"Oh, Riley! We're so excited to meet you!" one of them exclaims. "Your parents have told us so much about you!"

I find it difficult to believe that my parents were friends with these two precious little people, all kindness and generosity.

"Come, come!" Mrs. Covington says, taking my hand and tugging me to a hallway that goes past the kitchen. "Let me show you where you're staying."

"Uh, thank you, Mrs. Covington," I say, glancing behind me in mild panic to Lucy, the only one of the three who shows signs of sanity.

Lucy shrugs and mouths, "I was adopted."

I almost laugh, and then I'm surprised that there's a smile on my face within ten minutes of being here. I was pretty determined to hate everything, but I've managed to break another promise to myself. I don't think it's possible to hate this sweet little Mrs. Butterworth.

"Oh, sweetie, you can call me Merry Gene," she says, patting my arm and leaving a trail of flour behind. "You'll be staying with our Lucy--I hope that's okay?--and we got you a bed and a chest of drawers. After the hurricane last year, well, our finances aren't what they used to be...but you're welcome here, Riley. We're so happy to have you."

As Merry Gene goes on, she pulls me by the hand down the hallway to a narrow staircase and we climb up it to a small second story apartment. We enter a room that operates as both the living and dining rooms and I see a galley kitchen branch off and two bedrooms and a bathroom down the hall. I feel a stab of guilt--besides my college dorm, I've never lived in an apartment this small.

"Well, this is it!" Merry Gene declares, and Lucy appears at the top of the stairs behind us. "Lucy can show you your room." She wrings my hand and smiles at me, creases appearing at the corners of her eyes. "We're so happy to have you here for the summer."

I can't resist a smile at the woman's generosity. My own parents didn't want me, but this kind family was willing to take me in. Not only am I a failure, but also a reject.

Merry Gene heads back downstairs to return to the pizza shop, telling Lucy to make sure I'm comfortable. When her footsteps retreat down the stairs, Lucy smiles at me. "I'm sorry, she's a little...ov ereager. But here, let me show you where we're living."

I follow Lucy down the narrow hallway to a small room with a set of bunkbeds. Bunkbeds. This feels like my freshman year all over again. Lucy says she'll take the top bunk so I store my stuff under the bed and then sit on top of it, freshly made with seashell sheets. Once I sit down, I don't know what to do so I twiddle with the frayed hem of my jean shorts.

Lucy pulls up the singular chair of the room until our knees almost touch. "So," Lucy says with a short laugh, "I know this is kind of awkward. I don't really know much about you."

"Well, I just dropped out of college. That seems to be the most defining thing about me," I say with an apologetic grin.

She shrugs dainty shoulders. "I'm a law student but I work at my parents' pizza shop in the summers. Crap like that only defines you if you let it."

"Yeah, well, it forced me to come here, so I'd say it's pretty defining," I complain, then bite my tongue.

Lucy face falls, her dark eyebrows drawn together. "What do you mean?"

I try to backpedal, but it's too late. "I mean...okay, I didn't want to come here. I'll be honest. I'd much rather spend the summer with my parents, or--or do something that I chose."

"Well, just because you don't want to be here doesn't mean you have to let the opportunity go to waste." Lucy stands up and spins in a circle, and I have to lean back when her apron almost hits me in the face. She laughs, the sound of tinkling wind chimes. "It's the summer, we're at the beach, let's enjoy it."

And for a second--a brief second--I actually contemplate giving this summer a chance.

Fetch

R oss

Fetch. [fech]. The area of sea surface where the wind gener-
ates ocean waves.

"Ross!" Ivy squeals at the top of her lungs as soon as I open the
screen door to the house after my shift on the beach. A few seconds
later, she rounds the corner to the foyer at breakneck speed and at-
tacks me, clinging to my legs. "You're here! I've missed you so much!"

I ruffle her strawberry blonde curls and grin at her. "You know I
have to work during the summer, Iv."

"Why can't you stay home with me?" she asks, hands on her hips
and lips in a pout.

I understand her confusion. During the off-season, I stay home all
day and watch the kids while Dad works construction. Then I work
nights at the warehouse, loading trucks until I feel like my arms are
going to fall off.

I squat down and pull the crazy little seven year old into my arms. "I know, it's not fair, but you like hanging out with Mrs. May, right?"

Dorothy May, our next door neighbor, with her backyard full of bird feeders and ever-present chocolate buckeyes, watches the kids during the summer months while Dad runs the bike-rental business and I work as a lifeguard. They come home every night with chocolate painted on their faces, hopping up and down like a family of Easter bunnies.

"She's not as cool as you."

Awesome. I'm cooler than a 70 year old granny. "Of course I am," I tease her, standing back up and heading into the kitchen.

Dad sits at the kitchen table, scarfing down a sandwich of cold cuts, lettuce, and tomato. He raises a burly arm to wave at me.

"Hey, Ross," he says between bites, mayonnaise leaking out the corner of his mouth. "How was work?"

"No one died, so it went fine," I grumble.

He rubs his hands on his sweat-stained flannel shirt. "Can you stay home tonight? I'm going to head down to the pub with the guys."

Of course you are. Of course I get to stay home with the kids while he goes out and gets drunk on a Friday night. I didn't sign up to be a second parent just because I'm the oldest by over ten years.

"I was going to hang out with Earnest and Javier tonight. They just got here."

Dad shoves his chair back and it squeaks against the old linoleum. "You have all summer to hang out with them, and I'll take the kids to the beach tomorrow."

I scowl, scratching at my blonde curls. "Where you'll leave with me to watch while I'm lifeguarding. Thanks, Dad."

"Ross, don't give me that," he says, crossing his arms over his chest and raising a bushy salt and pepper eyebrow. "You know we have to work together here. For the kids. For your mom."

I draw in a sharp breath, my chest aching. Of course he's going to pull her into this. He knows that he can always use guilt to get me to pick up the extra slack around here. The kids deserve someone steady and loving in their lives, and that's obviously not my father.

I push past Dad. "Fine, Dad. You have fun."

His eyes follow me as I leave the kitchen and climb the steep stairs to the second floor, my footsteps creaking on the old floorboards. The upstairs has three tiny closet-sized bedrooms, one for the boys, one for Ivy, and one for me. I used to sleep on the couch downstairs, but then Dad started drinking and never made it up the stairs. I can't blame him for drinking or for wanting to spend a night forgetting about his life, but I still wish I wasn't alone in this, that I wasn't the one keeping us all afloat.

I hear soft footsteps behind me and look back to see Ivy's bright blue eyes following me up the stairs. "Are you and Dad fighting again?" she asks, raising her eyebrows and quirking her lips.

"Of course not." I sigh and take her hand, walking beside her to my room. "But guess what?"

"What?"

"I get to hang out with you tonight!" I exclaim, and she jumps up and down and squeals.

"Just me? No Mason or Sam?"

"Sorry, they have to hang out with us too."

"So you're babysitting us," she says, sticking her tongue out at me.

It's frustrating how perceptive a seven year old girl can be. "It's not babysitting if we eat pizza and watch a movie, is it?"

She puts a finger to her mouth. "Do I get to pick the movie?"

"Sure."

"Okay. We're watching Mulan." She turns and sprints out of the room. "Mason! Sam! Guess what? Ross says I can pick the movie!"

Her scream incites chaos and I hear the thunder of feet approaching the room. I sigh and lean back against my worn navy comforter. I love these kids with all of my heart, but babysitting a five year old, a seven year old, and a ten year old is not my idea of a good Friday night.

The thumping footsteps reach my door and redheaded Mason swings around, his green eyes huge. "Ivy gets to pick the movie? Why does Ivy get to pick the movie? I don't want to watch Mulan!" He screws his face up in disgust. "That's a girl movie."

I rub my temples, the exhaustion of staring at the ocean all day and then listening to screaming kids all night giving me a headache. "Because I said so. You can pick the next movie night."

Mason thinks for a moment, drawing his eyebrows together. "Fine. Do we get pizza?"

"Yep. And tell you what, you can pick the toppings," I say, hoping this will keep him happy.

"Pizza, pizza, pizza!" he yells, running back down the hallway with a guttural scream that sounds like it should come from the battlefield, not a five year old's bedroom.

Ivy disappears as well and I hear her talking to her American Girl doll in her bedroom next door. For all the chaos, I do love my siblings. I just wish I didn't feel like their father.

I pull my phone out of the pocket of my sweatpants and see an invite to hangout tonight in the group text between me, Earnest, and Javier. Crap. I send them a text and tell them I have to watch the kids, knowing they'll understand. They know about my family and they've even let the three kids tag along on some of our summer trips.

Still, I would kill to join them for our traditional bonfire on the beach to kick off the start of summer, but I can't. Dad's gotten worse lately; we used to share the responsibility of the three kids, but now it's all landed on me. I don't know what changed, but I feel tethered and asphyxiated. I'm 24 and I'm basically being both mother and father to the three kids.

Knuckles rap against the door frame and I look up. Sammy, with his glasses and carefully combed hair, stands in the doorway in a button-up shirt and khakis. He's ten, but he might as well be twenty for the way he acts.

"Ross, can you spare a moment of your time?" he says, pushing his glasses up on his nose.

"Sure, Sammy. What's up?"

He sighs. "It's Samuel. I've told you that before." I resist a grin--he's been Sammy since he was born, and there's no way I'm going to call him anything different now. "I fetched the mail today when I returned from Mrs. May's domicile."

"Did you get your magazine?" I ask in reference to Science Now!, the weekly magazine subscription I gave him for Christmas.

"Yes, the postmaster was kind enough to deliver it to me. There's a very informative article on neutrinos in this week's edition that I'm very much looking forward to reading."

I draw my lips together to keep from smiling. I love Sammy to death, but trying not to laugh when he talks like a college professor is the hardest thing I've ever had to do.

"That's great, Sammy. You'll have to tell me about it." Right before I go to bed.

I never hated school, but I wasn't exactly a star student and I haven't done any studying since I graduated from high school six years ago. I can't really relate to Sammy's thirst for knowledge; I'd rather rescue a 300 pound man from the riptide than read an article about neuro-whatevers.

"One more thing," he says, pulling something from his pocket. "You have received a letter from World Service International. May I inquire as to why they are sending you this correspondence?"

"No, you may not," I say, snatching the letter from his hand and closing the door in his face.

"I didn't tell you what toppings I would like on my pizza!" "Mason's picking this time," I yell back, staring down at the letter with shaking hands.

It came. I feel like a traitor even holding this letter. I didn't expect them to respond to my application so soon, so I'm guessing this has to be a rejection. I should have known. I don't have any experience--I've barely traveled outside of this island--and all I have is a high school diploma and six years of warehouse work experience.

Still, my heart pounds in my head like the beat of a drum. It's going to say no, I'm sure. But what if it doesn't? If it says no, nothing changes. No one has to know that I sent in my application. No one has to know I was considering leaving. But if it says yes...

Before I can even contemplate what that would mean, I tear open the envelope and pull out the letter. I scan the letterhead, but for a moment I struggle to even focus on the words before me.

Dear Mr. Montgomery...

Mr. Montgomery? I've never been called that before. I'm lucky they included my first name on the envelope or Dad might have opened it instead of me. That would have been bad. I can only imagine his reaction to learning that I'm leaving for nine months.

I force myself to read the first line of the letter.

Dear Mr. Montgomery,

We are pleased to inform you that you have been accepted into our World Service internship...

I drop the letter as soon as I read those words and sink onto my bed, running my hands through my hair. I'm in. I applied to their year-long service internship a month ago after a fight with Dad and a week spent babysitting. I wanted out--I still want out, but I applied on a frustrated whim. I never thought they'd actually accept someone like me into the program, but they did.

I curse under my breath and retrieve the letter, reading it ravenously. Now I have a choice. Do I leave at the end of the summer for a world-wide community service trip? Or do I stay at home, like I always have, and take care of my siblings?

All I want to do is see the world. See someplace outside of Long Beach Island, New Jersey. I want to see Brazil, France, Australia, Yemen, Bulgaria, Cambodia. But how can I leave Sammy, Ivy, and Mason with Dad? Who would take care of them, give them hugs, make sure they make it to school on time? How would our screwed up family even function without me? I crumple the letter into a ball and cram it under my matress. It doesn't matter if I want to go see the world for a year. If I left, Ivy, Mason, and Sammy would fall apart. Everyone else has already left them; I can't leave too.

Riptide

R iley

Riptide. [rip-tahyd]. A tide that opposes another or other tides, causing a violent disturbance in the sea.

All through high school and college, in every school and state I ever lived in, I always swam. It was my escape. In high school, I was on the varsity swim team. In college, I went to the regional conference for the back stroke. I sucked at everything else in life, but when I got into the tepid pool water and cut through it like nothing could stop me, I was extraordinary.

The nasty girls in my classes would always call me "that Army brat who can swim" which I guess is better than just "that Army brat." No matter what city we lived in, there was always a swimming pool and I could always dive into the cool water and leave my dark thoughts and fears behind me. Something about the rhythmic movement of my arms and legs pumping in unison stilled my mind and let me focus on one simple thing. Swimming.

Last night, I got out of girl talk with Lucy by saying that I was tired at 8:00 P.M. That definitely made waking up at six this morning significantly easier. I figure that if this summer isn't going to be a total waste of time, I might as well get my head in the right space with a swim. Merry Gene scheduled me for a shift at the pizza shop starting at noon which gives me time to put on my suit, head to the beach, swim a mile or so, and make it back in time to slave over the hot ovens in the kitchen. I haven't told her yet that I'm a horrific cook, but I figure she'll learn soon enough.

I slip out of my sheets on the lower bunk and clamber to my feet, tripping over my bag and making the floor creak. I sneak a glance up at Lucy on the top bunk--did I wake her up?

"Earnest--no!" she groans, rolling over. "Stop talking...about the Pythagorean theorem!" Another groan. "Let's...let's make out instead."

I cover my mouth to stifle my laugh--I'll have to ask Lucy about this later. I don't think I've ever heard the words "Pythagorean theorem" in the same sentence as "let's make out." I squat on the floor next to the bed and rifle through my bag until I find my bathing suit and a clean tank top and shorts. Then I sneak off the bathroom.

The tiny second-floor home is silent this early in the morning except for the ocean winds rattling the cedar shingles outside the window. The floor creaks a few times as I tiptoe to the bathroom, but no one rouses. The bathroom looks like it hasn't been renovated since the 80s with pink tiles on the wall and peeling linoleum. I change into my one-piece quickly, making sure I don't have a wedgie before I pull on my shorts and tank top. Even though I've detested this summer since I heard I was going to be sent to exile here, I'm still kind of excited to see the beach for the first time. We've lived a lot of places, but it's been a decade since I've seen the Atlantic Ocean, and I've never swam in anything but a pool before. My muscles yearn to give it a try.

I pull on flip-flops and pad softly down the hallway. In the kitchen, I leave a sticky note for the Covingtons to tell them I went down to the beach and I'll be back soon. Luckily, my parents didn't include an ankle monitor as part of my probation sentence, so I have a little bit of freedom.

I climb down the stairs and leave through the back entrance to the pizza shop, breathing in the salty air and tasting this new sense of freedom. Unlike yesterday afternoon, today Long Beach Island is sleepy and quiet. I see a few ambitious runners on the sidewalk with headphones in, but they ignore me. I can't imagine wanting to have headphones in when you could listen to the lapping of the waves and the seagulls chirping instead.

I cross the empty street and head for the beach. When I crest the top of the sand dune and see the ocean, I catch my breath. I've seen oceans in Europe and Asia and South America, but every single time, they take my breath away. My eyes trace the long coastline and the foaming waves that break onto the sandy beaches. I study the oscillating waters and the various colors that play across the surface--blues, greens, blacks--and the warm reflection of the morning sun on the water. I can see no one for miles except for an empty lifeguard stand an abandoned beach chair. It's just me.

Stripping out of my shorts and tank top, I drape them over a bench and check the mile marker so I'll remember where to come back to after my swim. I jog down the sand dune, feet slipping in the deep sand and lodging between my toes, and I start to laugh. There's no one here to tell me what a failure I am, badger me into becoming what they want me to be, force me into submission. I can be myself here, whoever that is. I kick the sand a few times, the granules brushing against my legs, and I lean down to look at a gorgeous shard of purple seaglass.

Okay, so maybe I was wrong. Maybe this summer isn't quite as bad as I anticipated it would be. True, I do have to spend the rest of my day flipping greasy pizzas and pretending to smile at annoying customers, but still. If I can spend my mornings here, I think I can put up with just about anything.

I skitter closer to the water and yelp when my toes finally make contact with the waves. Holy crap, that's cold. The water is icy, not yet warmed by the sun's rays, and goosebumps break out on my skin. I cross my arms over my chest and fight off a shiver, wishing I was wearing more than a one-piece Speedo. I walk along the beach for a while, lacking the nerve to jump into the waves, when I catch sight of something in the distance. I stop walking and strain my eyes.

Horses. I hold completely still and watch them run, a herd of horses with wild manes and salt-flecked coats of brown, black, and mottled gray. They gallop toward me, the wind blowing their untamed manes and tails in the wind. The lead horse skids to a stop when he sees me, whinnying and flaring his nostrils only a few hundred feet away. I watch him in awe, momentarily wondering if I should run away, but I can't. I'm entranced.

These wild horses are free; nothing keeps them in one location, so they go from place to place, itinerant travelers, nomads. These horses are a lot like me. Nothing ties them to one place or time; they flit to and fro where and when they want, making their own paths. But whereas my path has been haphazard and prone to trouble and disappointment, these wild horses are happy. The lead horse, a handsome bay, grows used to my silent company and nips at a few wild weeds growing on the sand dunes, watching me out of the corner of his dark eyes.

I'm jealous of a freaking horse. This horse is content with his lot, happy to wander where he pleases, but I've never been happy. I've always wanted something more, longing to finally settle in one location instead of living as a nomad all my days. An old granny in a checkered apron once told me that "home is where the heart is," and maybe that's my problem. I don't know where my heart is. It's not with my family; it's not with the very few friends I've managed to make or the places I've visited and lived in. Neither my heart nor I has a home.

I let out an exasperated sigh that reminds the horses that I'm here and that I don't belong with them. The first horse I saw rears onto his hind legs and lets out a whinny, calling the rest of the herd to follow him as they gallop away from me down the beach.

"Okay, enough," I mumble, falling into my old habit of talking to myself. "Stop feeling sorry for yourself and get in the freaking ocean."

I force myself to the edge of the waves again, inching into the water step by step. My toes curl up at the shock of the cold, but I force myself in. Once the water reaches my knees, I start to relax and I inch out further, squealing a little when one of the waves breaks against my chest. Finally, I dive in and paddle out to the point just past the breaking waves. I doggy paddle for a minute, catching my bearings and adjusting to the current. Unlike the pool, the sea has the power to push me back and forth, but I trust my experience to keep from being pulled out too far.

I take a breath and start to freestyle parallel to the beach. At first, my movements are stiff with cold and my legs struggle to flutter-kick, but eventually my muscles remember these movements and I glide through the water. The current takes some getting used to, but I like the way it feels. The water is as alive as I am, dancing with me as I weave through the waves. I flip over on my back and backstroke for a while, watching the seagulls that caw above me and a few whimsical clouds that mar the perfect blue sky. With each stroke, I swim farther and farther away from my troubled thoughts.

As I swim, my limbs start to grow sore from fighting against the current and my breath grows raspy. I check my Fitbit and see that I've swam a little less than half a mile, and I make a deal with myself that I'll finish the half mile and then head back to shore. I flip onto my stomach and push myself forward, straining every muscle to glide as quickly as I can through the water. My heart beats inside my head, pounding out a rhythm, and I draw in a quick breath on every stroke. I push myself to swim until every muscle screams for me to stop.

When I feel like my energy is spent, I doggy paddle for a minute and catch my breath. My Fitbit reads .57 miles--not bad for my first time swimming in the ocean. I look towards the beach and find I'm a little farther away than I expected, but life returns to my limbs with each huff of oxygen and I start to swim towards the beach.

That's when I feel the current--this time, it's not propelling me forward; it's pushing me back out to sea, fighting me from going back to the beach. I lengthen my arms and swim harder, trying to push against the tide, but I don't make any progress. Instead, the beach looks farther and farther away.

The pounding in my chest becomes frantic. I thought being alone was a good thing, but it's too early for the lifeguards and there was no one on the beach but the wild horses. If I can't get myself to shore...

In my panic, my head bobs underwater and I gulp a mouthful of ocean water, choking on it, and I paddle until I break free from the ocean's grasp. I cough out the water and try to paddle back to the beach, my arms and legs now flailing. It's not working. I'm getting nowhere.

Suddenly, a wave breaks on top of me and I'm shoved underwater again. The tide has me, it won't let go, and I'm alone. No one can rescue me, and as the water enters my lungs, I realize I can't save myself either.

Buoyancy

- -

R oss

Buoyancy. Noun. [boi-uhn-see]. The tendency of a body to float when submerged in water.

On the first day of summer, I have this tradition of going to watch the sun rise over the Atlantic. There's something reassuring about the sameness of the island: The sun always rises, the first day of summer always come, and the waves always lap rhythmically on the beach. Usually, this comforts me. Today, it ticks me off.

I sit on the first step down to the beach, fingers picking at a loose splinter of wood, and I watch the sun rise. It looks the same as it did last year, and every year before this. Last year, I brought Ivy to watch the sunrise with me in memory of the very first time I came here on the first day of summer with Mom, when I was five. I haven't missed a sunrise since. As I watch the sunrise today, however, it doesn't fill me with that same sense of peace. Instead, I feel like I'm stuck in the movie Groundhog's Day, living the same summer over and over again.

I'm tired of this same-old life I've lived for 24 years. My family has always lived on this island; my parents met here, fell in love here, got married here, and decided to raise their family here. And I do love the island, but nothing ever changes. I feel like I'm stranded inside a cage, but as I keep growing, it has become too small for me.

I walk down the wooden steps to the beach and sigh as my feet hit the sand. I strip off my t-shirt and leave it on a stake by the stairs and stretch my arms and legs. I walk to the edge of the water, my toes sinking into the cold sand, still wet from high tide, and I start to jog along the edge of the ocean, my feet pounding on the sand just beyond where the waves hit.

I can't get that letter from the world service internship out of my mind. I'm itching to get off the island, and this is my ticket out. It covers all the costs of travel and gives me a stipend to spend on food and housing in exchange for community service in whatever countries I live in. If it weren't for the three kids, I would be gone tomorrow.

My pace quickens and I lengthen my stride, my jog turning into a solid run. Every day of the year, except when the weather won't permit me, I come to the beach and run a few miles on the sand. With no tourists on the beach and no lifeguarding to be done, I'm free to actually enjoy the salty air and waves. I glance at the ocean every so often to see if I can catch a glimpse of the pod of dolphins that sometimes comes close to the shore in the morning, but I don't see anything but whitecaps.

As I run, I feel my chest start to heave and my breath quickens. I should probably slow down so I can run my usual three miles, but it feels so good to pour all of my energy into something, all my pent up frustration and this feeling of being stuck and paralyzed in a fate I don't want. On this beach, I'm free to run as far and as fast as I wish. Here, there's no drunk dad passed out on the couch. Ivy's not crying and asking when Mom's coming back. Mason isn't breaking everything in the house, acting out to get Dad's attention. Sammy isn't growing into an adult before his time. Out here, it's just me.

And the herd of wild horses running before me. I skid to a stop, sucking in harsh breaths that scrape my lungs, and watch as a handful of horses, manes and tails billowing in the wind, sprint past me. Something must have startled them, but as I look up the beach, I can see nothing except for a handful of sea gulls. I remain still as they run past me, so close that I can feel the thunder of their hooves on the sand. To them, I am nothing but a part of the beach.

Once they fade into the scenery of the beach, I continue on--this time, at a more manageable pace. As I go, I keep an eye out for whatever it was that disturbed the horses. I've only ever seen a handful of people on the beach this early, so I can't imagine what startled them.

I jog another mile, and that's when I see her. Or rather, I see a bobbing figure who's been pulled out to sea. I stop for a moment and stare, trying to figure out if it's a person or just a scrap of trash that floated to the surface of the water. When I see a hand emerge, waving frantically, I realize that this woman is drowning. I analyze her position for a minute--she's a few hundred feet from shore, I'm by myself, and I don't even have a life preserver. Crap.

I've rescued quite a few active drowning victims, but I'm usually not alone and I usually have the help of some sort of buoy. But here I am alone; I'll have to go out and swim her back to shore by myself. The girl flounders, trying to swim directly towards the shore, and I suddenly realize what's going on: She's caught in a rip current. If she keeps trying to swim to shore, it will just pull her out to sea even farther. I don't have any time to waste.

I sprint into the ocean, leaping over the waves until I'm so deep that they threaten to knock my feet out from under me. Then I dive into the water, the cold sending waves of shock through my body. I dive underneath the waves so they can't slow my progress and I feel my lifeguard training kick in. As I swim, I wonder who the heck this girl thinks she is. Swimming in the early morning, by herself, with no lifeguards on duty, beyond the breakers? Does she want to drown? Tourists.

Once I'm past the breakers, I resurface and draw in a few sharp breaths. Where'd she go? For a minute, I can't see any sign of her and I start to panic. Is she already gone? Did I lose her? I watch for a moment, and then I see it. A disturbance in the water--she's there, and she's still alive. She has to be.

I dive towards it, opening my eyes underwater despite the biting salt, and I see the girl's body, sinking into the ocean despite half-hearted kicks. I know she must be running out of oxygen, and she doesn't have much time. I reach for her and wrap my arms around her waist. In a few powerful kicks, I pull her to the surface and pant for air while I tread water.

"Hey, wake up! I got you, we're going to shore," I say, touching the girl's cold face. For a moment, nothing happens, and I'm afraid I've already lost her.

Then her eyes and mouth open and she draws in a huge, gasping breath. Her eyes, wide and alert, lock on mine, a pale almost translucent green, the color of seaglass. For a moment, I can do nothing but stare at her; then she starts to squirm in my grasp, flailing her arms and her legs in an attempt to break free. Her movements are wild and power and I struggle to keep us both afloat for a moment.

"Stop! What are you doing?" I yell. "I'm trying to rescue you!"

She calms down and I start to push her into shore, keeping my arms locked around her waist and positioning her so she can see the beach. Instead of trying to swim directly into shore, I swim parallel for a minute or two and then angle us back towards the beach once we're out of the rip current. As I carry her, my breathing becomes labored. She's not heavy, but carrying any weight in the ocean without the support of a flotation device is taxing, even for someone with as many years of experience as I have.

Her eyes stay opened, flicking from my face to the beach, and she continues to gasp for breath. A few times, she looks like she's going to speak, but she's at least smart enough to save her breath. What kind of girl swims by herself, starts to drown, and then tries to push away the guy who saves her? Between the exertion and rage, my blood boils and I break out in a sweat despite the icy temperature of the water. Four. More. Strokes.

Finally, my feet touch the stand and I struggle to my feet. I lift the girl out of the water into my arms like a child and stagger out of the ocean. When we reach the beach, I lay her none too gently on the sand and then collapse next to her, out of breath from the run and the rescue. I sit with my arms resting on my knees and gasp for breath, checking to make sure she can breath. Her lips have turned blue but she continues to draw shattering breaths into her lungs. For a few minutes, she lies flat on her back, sucking in air and shaking from the cold.

"Are you alright?" I finally ask her, eying her pale, freckled complexion made even icier by the cold.

She sits up and hugs her knees to her chest, glaring at me from her wild, gorgeous green eyes. "I...I'm perfectly fine," she hisses between chattering teeth.

As if on cue, she turns away from me and hurls onto the beach, puking up every drop of saltwater she swallowed. She runs the back of her hand across her mouth and curses lightly.

"You're not fine," I growl, "you would have drowned if I hadn't been here."

"I wouldn't have drowned," she answers, rolling her eyes and pulling her long legs closer to her chest. "I swam for a first division school in college. I know how to swim."

"Well, you've obviously never swam in the ocean before or you would have known how to avoid a riptide," I bite back.

I chide myself internally for letting this uppity tourist get under my skin. Maybe it's the untamed look in her eyes or the way her swimsuit shows off the muscles in her slender legs. Whatever it is, she makes me want to throw her back in the ocean and leave her to drown.

"I'm a good swimmer--a great swimmer," she says, but this time I hear the puzzlement in her voice. Maybe she recognizes how close she was to drowning.

I stand up, kicking sand onto her as I rise. "Yeah, well, in that case, sorry for rescuing you."

"You want a thank you, is that it?" She stands next to me, arms still wrapped around her. Her skin is so pale and icy that she looks like she's going to turn into an icicle in front of me. "My knight in shining armor," she coos, batting her eyelashes at me.

I sigh--what difference does it make if she thanks me or not? Absolutely none. "Here, let me walk you back to your beach house. You need to find your beach towel and get warmed up."

I reach out a hand to provide her support--I can tell she's close to collapsing again, wavering on her feet. Of course, she ignores me and stalks away, tripping in the sand as she goes.

"I can take care of myself."

I watch her go, her lithe form in only a black Speedo and her footsteps faulty. Maybe I should go after her, but how am I supposed to help someone who refuses to let me touch her? I wasn't trying to play hero; I was trying to save her life.

"See you later, princess," I mumble under my breath as she walks away.

~~~~~

And Ross and Riley meet! What do you think of their first encounter? I hope to have another chapter published soon. I'm excited to see Riley's reaction to Ross's daring rescue :)

If you're enjoying, please vote and comment, and thanks for reading!

~ Hannah

Life Preserver

R iley

Life preserver. Noun. [lahyf pri-zurv-er]. A buoyant jacket, belt, or other like device for keeping a person afloat.

What's worse than having to be rescued from almost drowning the ocean? Being rescued by a really hot guy who isn't wearing a shirt. What's worse than that? Having said hot guy yell at me for being stupid enough to swim in the ocean alone.

I am the living, walking definition of mortification.

Just when I thought this summer was taking a turn for the better, I get myself caught in a riptide and almost die. A tiny part of me wishes I would have drowned instead of having to face smug little Lifeguard Larry and his six pack. I storm off the beach in a rage, tripping through the sand and shivering as I go. I think it's safe to say I learned my lesson. No more swimming in the ocean for me.

I find my tank top and shorts on the bench where I left them and I tug them on, still shaking. The skin under my fingernails is turning blue and I feel like I just swallowed a few gallons of saltwater. Delightful.

When I get back to A Pizza the Action, I'm happy to find the Covingtons aren't awake yet. I shed my clothes and climb into the shower, letting the hot water finally raise my body temperature so I don't feel like I have hypothermia anymore.

I can still hear the words of Lifeguard Larry ringing in my ears. "See you later, princess."

I sincerely hope that he's just an over-valiant tourist with a hero complex who's here for the week, but knowing my luck, he won't be. This island's pretty big though; maybe if I avoid the beach in the mornings, I can also avoid his know-it-all frown and blue eyes the color of the ocean.

A few hours later, I'm awoken from my post-shower nap by Lucy singing my name. "Ri-ley, Ri-ley! It's time to wake up!"

It feels like my one and only week of summer camp all over again. "What?" I grumble, trying to sit up and banging my head on the bunk above me.

I am way too old for bunkbeds.

"A Pizza the Action opens in a half hour and we need to be there in fifteen minutes to get everything ready. Remember? You're working today?"

I groan and flop back onto the bed. If I have fifteen minutes, I calculate that I can sleep approximately thirteen more minutes and still make it in time.

"We're getting everything ready. Don't you want something to eat before we start working?"

"Not especially."

Lucy sighs and grabs my arm, pulling me off of the bed. I land on the floor with a bang, bruising my tailbone and my pride at once. She's stronger than she looks.

"Get up! We have a great day ahead of us. Saturdays are always our busiest day!"

I moan again, gingerly rising from my supine position on the floor. "And that's supposed to make me want to work?"

"It'll be a blast! Today's the first day of summer. How can it not be fantastic?" Nothing I say can sour Lucy's ever present cheer. She beams at me, her eyes twinkling into half moons. "So get dressed and let's get going. You have to wear pants past the knees and a t-shirt, plus an apron." She throws an apron on my bed and bounces out of the room, humming a Christmas song as she goes. I dig through my bag and find a pair of capris and a ratty gray t-shirt. I hold up the apron and grimace. Not only does it have an embroidered pizza and the name "A Pizza the Action" on the front, but it's cardinal red. Everyone will know that I'm employed in slave labor at A Pizza the Action.

I tie the apron around my waist and then knot it in the front since I'm pretty sure this apron was designed for someone who eats way too much pizza himself. I trudge to the kitchen where Merry Gene Covington is cleaning up cereal bowls from the breakfast I missed.

As if on cue, my stomach grumbles. I already swam almost a mile and nearly drowned today, and I haven't eaten anything.

"How'd you sleep, sweetie?" she asks me. I mumble something incoherent and she tosses me a granola bar with a wink. "Just in case you're hungry. I know some days it's a miracle that I don't steal a slice of every pizza we bake because I get so hungry!" She cackles and bustles down stairs to the already waiting crowd.

I munch on the granola bar by myself in the kitchen; I can hear the sounds of waiting customers already anticipating the hot pizza goodness of the restaurant. Who eats pizza at ten in the morning? Probably the same person who made this giant apron.

When I finish the bar, I stumble down the stairs and enter the back door into the kitchen. The three Covingtons are already at work; Lucy mans the cash register and counts out ones, fives, and tens as well as a few handfuls of quarters. Then she heads to the tables and wipes them down one by one. In the kitchen, Merry Gene rolls out pizza dough, slathers on the tomato sauce, and then sprinkles generous portions of toppings on top. Ronald, also known as Mr. Covington, mans the pizza ovens, filling them with pizzas, strombolis, quesadillas and every other Italian delicacy. His bald head is red and sweat already drips down his face. The unnamed pimply teenager I met yesterday is at work in the back room, digging through an industrial sized refrigerator and fetching the various toppings. I see onion, bacon, sausage, pineapple, and more. Even though it's early and I'm already determined to hate this job, my stomach still growls at the smell of the cooking pizza.

"Welcome to A Pizza the Action, Riley!" Merry Gene cries, beaming at me with round cheeks. "We're so happy you're working here this summer."

"I promise the benefits are good," Ronald interjects. "We were voted best pizza on the island, and you'll never guess what we're having for lunch." He wags his bushy eyebrows and displays a pizza with a Vanna White wave.

"I never would have guessed," I mumble, but I can't keep from smiling. I've never met two people who love pizza more.

"Since it's your first day and just so happens to be our first day of summer, I won't have much time to train you on how to make the pizzas or work the register, so, you're on dish duty!" Merry Gene announces as if I just won the lottery.

She tosses a wet, sudsy rag at me and I catch it, some of the filthy water splattering onto my beautiful apron. "Lucky me," I grumble and make my way to the huge stainless steel double sink.

Even though it's only 9:30, the sink is already full of dishes--pizza platters, silverware, plastic bowls that hold pizza toppings. I turn on the faucet and a spray of hot water splatters me instantly. Crap. I grab the hose and pull it loose, directing it at the dishes instead of myself. Unfortunately, it's too late and I'm already soaked for the second time in one day. At least this time I didn't need to be rescued.

At 10:00 A.M., the front doors open and a rush of enthusiastic customers come in. In a bizarre turn of luck, I don't have to deal with them thanks to my position as Official Dish Washer. I spend the morning and early afternoon washing dishes, drying them, returning them to their homes, and then washing the next set. I fall into this routine, my hands turning into shriveled prunes and sweat pouring from my body as the entire kitchen heats up thanks to the ovens.

Around two, Merry Gene touches my shoulder and offers me a towel and a piece of pizza. Apparently this is my lunch break. I collapse onto a spare chair and shovel the entire slice of cheese pizza into my mouth. Between the swim and slave labor, I've worked up an appetite. I'm typically more of a salad and fruit sort of person, but today the greasy pizza hits the spot. I even go back for seconds.

After my brief lunch break, I spend the afternoon wiping down tables and picking up all the trash our customers found themselves unable to throw away themselves. That evening, around four, we do it all over again. It's ten o'clock until all the customers are gone, everything is cleaned and put away, and we eat the leftover food.

As we trudge up the stairs to fall into our beds, I feel something strange: contentment. I realize that I've never really had a job before. Sure, in college I was a part-time swim coach for a few semesters, and I had a brief stint as a waitress in high school (for three months before we moved again), but this is the first job I've really had. And as mundane and redundant as washing dishes is, I enjoyed being part of the Covingtons' pizza shop. Not to mention the benefits, courtesy of Mr. Covington. I understand why they were voted best pizza shop on the island, and I'll be lucky if I haven't gained fifteen pounds by the end of the summer.

Once I'm upstairs, I trudge into my room and find my discarded cell phone. Zero notifications. I shouldn't be surprised; I've never had long-term friendships, so there's no one to text me and ask how my first day went. Still, I thought maybe my mom would at least send me a text. That's a mom sort of thing to do, like taking a first day of school picture or chaperoning the first prom. My mom never did any of those things, and I never want to prom, so I guess we're too far from normalcy for me to expect something like a simple "how was your day?" text.

I text her to see how the U.A.E. is, and despite the time difference, she texts me back. It's already 6:00 A.M. tomorrow in Dubai, and she's awake and getting ready for the day, which means putting on three layers of makeup and a dress that shows off the body Weight Watchers gave her. She sends me a picture of the Burj Khalifa, a huge tower in Dubai, and says that she wishes I was there. The words send a pang of loneliness through me. I wish I were there too. Exploring Dubai with my mom sounds far superior to nearly dying in the ocean and spending hours and hours working in a pizza shop.

I pull up Mom's number and call her. "Hello, darling!" she answers, sounding like Audrey Hepburn from My Fair Lady.

"Hey, Mom."

"Is something wrong, Riley? I have quite a lot to do today."

"How's Dubai?"

"Oh, just fantastic. Your father and I both wish you were here."

"Oh yeah?"

"Of course. But I'm sure you'll love spending the summer with the Covingtons and their daughter. If I remember correctly, they were quite a...traditional sort of family."

You mean exactly the opposite of ours?

"Yeah, I just spent ten hours working in their pizza shop."

This makes Mom pause. "Well, I'm glad you're learning the value of hard work. Your father and I were much too easy on you growing up."

"Are you sure I can't come and visit you and Dad? Just for a weekend?" I haven't seen them since Christmas, so I feel like this is a valid request. Plus, I've never been to Dubai.

"Honey, I just don't think that's financially possible."

I snort, picturing the new Prada ball gown she bought a few weeks ago. I'm pretty confident money has nothing to do with it. They just don't want me there.

"Please? You basically have me doing slave labor here for the summer. The least you could do is let me come see you sometime this year."

"I'm afraid that's not an option, Riley. You understand that this a punishment for you dropping out of college, don't you?"

Emotion wells in my throat and I try to swallow it down. There's no use getting upset about something I've known my entire life: My parents care more about their jobs and lifestyle than they do about their daughter. They say they sent me here because I dropped out of Cornell, but it's really because I'm an obstacle. They never wanted me in the first place; I was an accident, an oops baby, and stranding me on an island in New Jersey was the best way to get rid of me for a summer.

"Of course I understand, Mom. Sorry to be such an inconvenience."

I end the call and flop on the bottom bunk, tears welling in my eyes. Lucy enters a few seconds later and stares at me for a few moments. I wonder if she overheard our conversation, but then I realize it doesn't matter. All she would do is feel bad for me, and I don't need her pity.

Sessile

R^{oss}

Sessile. Adjective. [ses-il]. Permanently attached; not free to move about.

One of my favorite things about summer is the beach bonfires. Almost every night, a group of lifeguards and islanders gather on the beach for a roaring bonfire, accompanied by hot dogs and s'mores. It seems kind of ridiculous that after spending the entire day on the beach we would want to come back here at night, but no matter how tired I am of the island, I will always love the ocean. In the evening, the temperature drops and the reflection of the moon glitters across the dark waters. If we're lucky, we can even catch a glimpse of the stars.

"Rossy, is Javier gonna be at the bonfire tonight?" Ivy asks from beside me, tugging on my hand as the four of us make our way to the beach.

I raise my eyebrows and laugh. "Javier? Yeah, probably. Why?"

"Oh, no reason."

I laugh as we make our way to the edge of the dunes, the bonfire glowing against the black night. My muscles are sore from rescuing that girl in the ocean yesterday and from hours spent in the lifeguard chair, but I feel all of my stress fade away when my feet touch the sand. As soon as Mason sees the fire, he sprints toward it, yelling like a banshee. I should probably be concerned that he'll try to run through the fire or go for a swim, but I know someone will stop him. The islanders and lifeguards are a family, and we watch out for each other. Plus, everyone knows my family's story and they try to look out for the Montgomery kids when they can.

Ivy stays beside me and starts to chatter about something related to her American Girl doll, and Sammy bends down to look in the sand for a "complex organism he desires to examine." Some days I feel like I live with Bill Nye the Science Guy.

A dark shadow turns in front of the fire. "Montgomery! It's about time."

Javier lopes toward us, his white smile the only thing visible in the dark. Even though Javier, Earnest, and I all work as lifeguards, since we've been here for a while, our boss spreads us out along the beach. We don't see each other very often during the days except for brief conversations during ATV patrols of the beach.

"Hey, Javi," I say, clasping hands with him.

He kneels down in front of Ivy and gives her a smile. "Hey, my favorite girl's finally here! How are you, Ivy?"

She ducks her head and grins at him, tugging on a blond wave. "Hi, Javi."

He clutches his chest. "What, no hug for me?"

That brings the end of Ivy's momentary lapse of timidity; she jumps towards him and nearly knocks him back into the sand. Javier laughs, picking her up and carrying her to the fire as I follow him, hollering for Sammy to come with us.

Javier carries Ivy to where Earnest sits in the sand, his cellphone in hand. "Hey, Ernie," I say as Javier, Ivy, Sammy and I have a seat. Mason is running around the beach terrorizing seagulls; I let him be. At least he's not terrorizing babies and toddlers like last year. "Who you texting?" "Who do you think?" Javier interjects.

"Lucy's not here yet?" I ask, scanning the crowd for Lucy's shoulder length black hair and constant smile.

"Nah, she's on her way. Had to work late at the pizza shop."

My stomach grumbles when I think about the Covingtons' pizza. It's by far the best pizza on the island, and the Covingtons are some of my favorite islanders. I'm going to have to drop by soon.

"So Ross, I hear you have a story for us," Javier taunts in a singsong voice.

"Oh yeah, didn't you have to rescue some girl yesterday?" Earnest says, setting down his phone.

As if I want to relive that. "Yeah, it was no big deal."

"Of course it was!" Javier says, slugging me in the arm as I sit in the sand, leaning back on my hands.

I touch Ivy's shoulder. "Ivy, why don't you go play with Jemma?"

Jemma, one of the Islander girls, has a few Barbies out on the sand and Ivy happily runs over to join her. Sammy has whipped a science magazine out of nowhere and is completely immersed in it, and Mrs. Sanchez gives Mason a s'more. That'll make for a fun sugar high here in a few minutes.

"So? What happened?"

"There's not much to tell. I was running on the beach around six or six thirty and I saw something out in the water, past the breakers. I thought it was a piece of trash, a plastic bag or something, but it was a girl."

Javier leans forward, resting his arms on his knees. "By girl, do you mean she was our age or Ivy's age?"

I close my eyes briefly, picturing the girl's round green eyes and slender figure. "Our age."

"Was she hot?"

Earnest glares at Javier. "Go on, Ross."

"She was trying to swim straight toward the shore through a riptide and it was pulling her under. There wasn't anyone else on the beach, so I had to go after her myself."

"Zero to hero," Earnest comments.

"It sucked, actually," I say with a low laugh. "She kept fighting me and I had to haul her back to shore. I thought we were both going to pass out by the time we finally made it to the beach."

"Let me guess. After you gave her mouth to mouth, she thanked you profusely for being her knight in shining armor and pledged to love you till the day she dies."

I roll my eyes. I picture her batting her sea glass eyes at me and saying those exact words. My knight in shining armor. Except the words were dripping with sarcasm.

"Not quite. She got mad at me and stormed away."

Ernie glances up from his cell phone. "She got mad? Why? You saved her life?"

I sigh. This girl is still under my skin, and I don't even know her name. "I have no idea. I would have left her there if I'd realized she would be so much trouble."

Javier lays back on the sand, staring up at the sky. "You still didn't answer the most important question. Was she hot?"

An image of the girl comes to my mind, standing in front of me with her round, flashing eyes, angry scowl, long legs. "Yeah," I answer. "She was hot."

Javier hoots and slaps me on the leg, but I just grin. There's not much else to say. The girl was annoying even if she was hot, and besides, she's probably a tourist who'll be gone in a few days anyways. At least it makes for a good story.

A shadow swoops in from behind us and wraps its arms around Earnest. "Hey, guys!" Lucy chirps, smiling at Javier and me as she sits next to Earnest, their legs entwining in the sand.

"Hey, Lucy Liu. It's about time you got here," Javier quips. "Ernie's barely looked up from his phone waiting for you."

She sighs and snuggles up to Earnest like they're an old married couple. "A Pizza the Action was crazy today, like it always is on Saturdays. I couldn't leave until now."

I glance down at my watch--it's already after ten. I'm going to need to take the kids back and put them to bed soon. So much for a fun night with friends.

"How was work?" Earnest asks, staring at her like she's an oasis in the desert.

"Oh, not bad," Lucy says, brushing her smooth hair behind her ear. "We have extra help this summer. This girl, I guess her parents knew mine way back before they adopted me, is staying with us for the summer. She dropped out of Cornell or something so her parents sent her here."

"To work at a pizza shop?" I question. I like pizza and all, but that doesn't sound like the ideal summer job for a girl who's smart enough to go to Cornell.

"She gets to live with us for free if she works at the shops."

Javier with his one track mind asks, "So is she hot?"

Lucy wrinkles her small nose. "Javi, come on. She's...nice, I guess."

I raise my eyebrows and laugh. Lucy never says a bad word about anyone. "She must be really awful."

"She's not so bad. She just...well, she doesn't want to be here. Last night I heard her trying to convince her parents to let her visit them. I guess they haven't seen each other since Christmas."

I should probably count my blessings. For better or worse, I have Dad to deal with every day. I wonder if I would miss him if I took the global internship, but I know better. I would feel free without him dragging me down with his carelessness and irresponsibility.

"Where are her parents from?" Earnest asks.

"Well, I'm not really sure. They lived here for a while, but now they're in Dubai."

Dubai. I search the map I've memorized from hours of imagining where I would go if I could. Dubai's in the United Arab Emirates in the Middle East, a beautiful country with stunning landscape and magnificent architecture. If I had the chance, I'd rather be in Dubai too.

Javier whistles. "They must have some money."

Again, Lucy shrugs. "I don't know. I guess her dad's some big shot in the Army or something. They've lived a bunch of places."

I feel a sting of jealousy for a girl I've never even met. This hunger inside me to travel and see the world is so ravenous that it's swallowing my enjoyment of the summer and time with friends and family entirely. These summer nights used to be vibrant and fun, but they've become lackluster in comparison to where I could be. In a couple months, if I choose to take the internship.

Mason wanders over to me, chocolate smeared across his freckled face and eyes half-closed. I sigh and stand, picking him up.

"I guess that's my cue." I wave goodbye to Javier, Earnest, and Lucy and find Ivy still playing with Barbies in the sand. "See you guys later."

I take Ivy's hand and call Sammy, and we trudge home in the dark of night. My mind is lost imagining what the girl at the Covingtons' has experienced. What countries has she visited? What landmarks and museums has she seen? What kind of people has she met? Does she know different languages?

"Rossy?" Ivy calls next to me and I subjugate my dreams of escape. The kids need me, and that's why I have to stay.

"What's up, Ivy?"

"I've reached a decision," she says. "I'm going to marry Javier."

Before I can stop myself, I break out laughing. "Oh, are you now?"

"Yes. I've decided. We're going to get married next summer and have three children."

She's way too young for the birds and the bees talk. "Well, you'll have to talk to Javier about that."

"He told me I was his favorite girl."

I laugh and tug Ivy to keep up with me. She's half asleep as she walks, sandaled feet dragging on the sidewalk. When we get home, Mason is asleep on my shoulder, drool dripping from his mouth onto my t-shirt, and Ivy is only half awake as well. When I find Dad asleep on the couch, I sigh and take the kids upstairs. Sammy puts himself to bed while I help Ivy and Mason change and tuck them in.

After they're asleep, I go downstairs and clean up after Dad. There are a handful of empty beer cans on the floor next to the couch and the TV still plays Wheel of Fortune. I throw the trash away, turn off the TV, and stare at Dad for a minute. How could I leave the kids here with him? He's barely capable of taking care of himself and it's a miracle he has a job. I'm going to be stuck here until Mason, the youngest of the three kids, is out of high school. Plus, how am I supposed to give them better lives than I had if I don't save up to help them pay for college? My head starts to ache and I climb into bed, hoping sleep will take away this discontent that aches in my bones.

As I lean back onto the same twin-sized bed I've slept in for the past 24 years, my feet dangling over the end, I stare up at the ceiling.

When I was eight, I glued a map of the entire world to the ceiling. I decided that every time I went somewhere, I would mark it with a pushpin so I could keep track of the thousands of places I visited. I'd read Treasure Island and Robinson Crusoe and The Swiss Family Robinson. I kept imagining all these adventures i would have and places I would see. But all my dreams were for nothing.

The map is still empty.

Turbulence

R iley

Turbulence. Noun. [tur-byuh-luh-ns]. The haphazard secondary motion caused by eddies within a moving fluid.

"Riley!"

I bury my nose deeper in my book, hoping Merry Gene will leave me in peace.

"Riley, honey, can you hear me?"

Why does she have to be so nice? I lay my book down on the front counter next to the cash register and turn around with a sigh.

"Loud and clear. What's up?"

"Oh, I'm sorry, I didn't mean to interrupt your reading! What book is it?" She approaches the counter and picks up my paperback, examining the cover. "The Perks of Being a Wallflower. Hmm, what a strange title. I've never heard of a wallflower, but then again, I've never been much of a gardener." I bite my lip to stifle a giggle. "Do you like to read? I'm quite a reader myself. I like a good romance once in awhile to heat things up with Ronald and me. I don't like to let our marriage get old and stale, if you know what I mean?"

Merry Gene gives me an angelic smile and I shudder. I know exactly what she means; I mentally calculate the distance from the bedroom I share with Lucy to their bedroom. Too close. Far too close. I back away from the counter and tell myself to never ask to borrow a book from her.

"Did you need me to help with something?" I say, willing to scrub the floors with my toothbrush if that means I can avoid this conversation.

"You don't mind? I know things are slow here today, so I wanted to restock and clean a little bit." I try to give her give her one of Lucy's trademark smiles, something to convince her I'm excited to be here, but we all know I'm terrible at pretending. "Sure. What can I do?"

"Would you mind refilling the ketchup and mustard bottles and then the salt and pepper shakers? The refills are on the bottom shelf in the storage room."

"Sure."

Merry Gene gives me a graceful smile as I trudge to the back room and I know she wants me to feel at home here, but I'm still slave labor. I can't get my conversation with Mom out of my head. No matter how many ways she tries to disguise it, Mom and Dad don't want me around. If I'm honest with myself, I know that they've never wanted me at all. I'm accidental baggage that they've shoved off on someone else.

I glance over the shelves in the back room and find the mustard and ketchup dispensers and haul them out to the restaurant part of the pizza shop. The bottles sit on the trash can next to the napkins and I trudge over, unscrew the lid on the mustard bottle, and refill it.

I guess I shouldn't complain about living here for the summer. I get to stay in the same place for three months, which by my standards is a pretty long time. And now I have endless hours of refilling ketchup dispensers and washing dishes to spend thinking about my very uncertain future. The thing is, I don't want to think about my plans. Any money I have is from my parents, so I don't have the funds to do what I want--whatever that is. They'll support me if I choose to return to Cornell in the fall, but I feel like it's too late for that. Maybe if I studied something other than business I'd like it, but I have no idea what my passion is. I hate the idea of working a monotonous nine to five job. If I ever settled into a job, it would have to be something I cared a lot about.

The only job I've ever really enjoyed was the summer I spent teaching kids to swim at the YMCA. There was an adorable, bespectacled kid named Bartholomew who I became friends with. He was an Army brat just like me, and I worked one-on-one with him for hours. It was more than just teaching him swimming; we talked about life, and how hard it is to make friends. Is it weird that an eight year old Army brat was one of the best friends I ever had?

Still, I'm not sure I'd be able to make it as a professional swim coach. Not after my recent dunk in the ocean. I could go back to Cornell for something else, but I'm not sure what I'd major in if or

I'd even make it another year. I might quit again on a whim and just walk away, like I've done from every other challenge in my life. With my family's many relocations, I've learned to just leave when things get hard. That's pretty much what I did with Cornell, and that's what I'll do here when the summer ends.

"Excuse me."

My entire body stiffens as soon as I hear the guy behind me. The last time I heard this voice, it was telling me how stupid I was for swimming in the ocean. You've got to be kidding me. As I go rigid with shock, I squeeze the ketchup bottle in my hand and the slimy red liquid squirts all over me, covering my gorgeous red apron and dripping down my face. Just when I thought I couldn't be any more embarrassed.

I reach for a napkin and wipe off my face as I turn around to glare at the guy behind me. It's my knight in shining armor from the beach a few days ago; of course he would stumble into our tiny little pizza shop, and of course I would be refilling the ketchup bottles when he came in. Just my freaking luck.

As I turn, I stare up into those ocean-blue eyes that I saw for the first time while I was choking on saltwater and flailing my limbs like a maniac. He's just as attractive in person, and the jersey t-shirt hanging over his torso brings a flashback of infuriatingly perfect washboard abs. His eyebrows shoot up when he sees me and then he grins.

"Well, hey," he says, taking me in with a sweep of his eyes.

My face turns red right away and for a half-second I'm grateful for the smattering of ketchup to disguise my blush.

"You, uh, have something right there." A half smile climbs up his tanned face as he touches his own cheekbone.

"Crap."

I turn away from him quickly, grabbing napkins and scouring my face. He's here. He's legitimately standing in front of me. I toss the reddened napkins into the trash can and remove my filthy apron, fleeing to the kitchen. What the heck am I supposed to say to this guy? My mortification has faded enough for me to realize I owe him a thank you, but after the exploding ketchup, how can I even face him?

"You're looking a little better than the last time I saw you," he says, following me to the checkout counter.

I turn around to seem him lounging against the counter on his elbows with a half-grin on his face.

I roll my eyes. "What a compliment."

"The ketchup's a nice touch."

I glare at him. Does he seriously not know when to stop? "Can I get you something?" He completely ignores me. "So you're the girl who's staying at the Covingtons for the summer?"He's heard of me? I shouldn't be surprised. The island's small so I'm sure news travels fast among the locals. I wonder what he's heard. Army brat. College dropout. Stuck-up rich kid. I've heard it all before.

"That's me," I say, opening up my book and tossing the bookmark on the counter. Maybe he'll go away if I ignore him.

"Welcome to Long Beach," he says. "I figured you were a tourist."

I fasten my eyes on the page in front of me, but my face still heats up. "Thanks, it was a great welcome. I love being hauled out of the ocean like a beached whale."

To my surprise, he laughs. "I'm guessing that's as close to a genuine thank you as I'm going to get."

I bite my lip to keep from smiling--the fact that he refuses to be offended by my sarcasm is slightly endearing. Just slightly.

"I'd say that's a pretty accurate guess."

I lower my book to make eye contact with him again, and for a half-second, I admit to myself just how attractive he is. His hair is curly, blonde, and untamed, bleached by a summer spent under the sun. He's tan and obviously muscular, probably just so he can drag half-dead chicks out of the water. His smile is what draws me in, though. It's crooked and effortless, and his eyes are kind. I like him much more now than I did when he was screaming at me for my horrible swimming. Granted, that's a pretty low standard.

He leans against the counter, looking up at me for a second, and then grabs my bookmark. It shows the Cathedral of Notre Dame lit up at night. Mom, Dad, and I vacationed there one year--it was a vacation, but Dad spent half the time working. Still, I got to see the Cathedral, the Eiffel Tower, and a thousand other tourist sites while we were there.

"You've been to France?"

The wonder in his voice makes me give him a double take. "Yeah, while I was in high school."

"Dang. I've always wanted to go there." He runs his finger along the bookmark and sighs.

My cynical facade calls and I smile. "Honestly, it was incredible. Everyone should visit Europe at least once in their lives."

My words make him stiffen and he drops the bookmark. "Yeah, well, not all of us has that chance." He heaves a sigh. "Have you traveled a lot?"

I shrug. "I'm an Army brat. I've moved eighteen times counting this summer and I traveled a lot with my family for my dad's work while I was growing up."

Why am I telling this guy my life story? I know I should shut up and get back to my important role as ketchup refiller, but the way he leans against the counter and looks at me, drinking in every word I say, makes me want to tell him more.

"I have to tell you, I'm pretty jealous. I'd love to travel." I want to ask him why he doesn't, but I realize I don't even know his name. I definitely don't know him well enough to ask him about his hopes and dreams even though I find myself curious about him.

"Yeah, well, don't be too jealous." I grin at him. "I'm still stuck here talking to you."

He looks up at me and matches my grin so we look like two idiots beaming at each other.

"That must be awful."

"You don't know the half of it."

Tidal Power

R oss

Tidal power. Noun. [tahyd-l pou-er]. Electricity made from the moving waters of the tides.

I literally can't stop smiling. This girl's arrogant, rude, sarcastic, uppity, everything I usually hate about mainlanders, but I still can't stop smiling. There's something so alive about her that I can't look away.

Every time she meets my gaze, her eyes crackle and burn with energy. They're round and green, so large and haunting that they seem to take up her entire face. I feel a little better when my gaze drops from her eyes to her mouth and I see she's smiling like an idiot too.

I don't know her name, but I know that she's discontent, that she's traveled her whole life and never settled down, that she's a wild, restless soul. I don't even know her name, but I know there's something in her that's just like me.

"So did you come in here just to keep me from doing my important duty as the Queen of the Ketchup?" she asks, rolling back on her heels and squeezing the edge of the counter.

"Believe it or not, I came in here for pizza."

Her face deadpans. "No way."

"I just needed a pizza the action."

I cringe at my own terrible joke, but she laughs, contorting the myriad of freckles dancing across her tiny nose.

"That was so cheesy," she retorts and I slap my face with the palm of my hand. "So what can I get you, knight in shining armor? A slice of humble pie?" She picks up the order notebook and readies her pen, her tongue against her lip in faux concentration.

I grin at the girl's easy wit and I debate teasing her more about the near-drowning debacle, but I find myself wanting to stay on her good side.

"How about two pizzas, one with pepperoni and one with plain cheese?"

"Two pizzas?" She grins at me again. "You better be careful or you'll lose that beach bod."

Though her words were meant as a slam, I see a blush tingle across her face as she realizes what she said and I'm way happier than I should be that she already checked me out. At least I have one thing going for me.

"They're not all for me," I explain with a laugh. "They're for the kids."

Her eyebrows shoot up. "Kids?"   Now it's my turn to flush red. "Not--not mine. My dad's. My brothers and sisters."

She laughs and winks at me as she turns to order the food. "Coming right up."

She saunters to the back room, leaving her book and bookmark open on the counter. I watch as she leaves--a little more closely than I probably should--and try to connect what Lucy said about this girl with what I see. Lucy seemed to think she was lonely and angry about spending her summer here, and I can see that, but there's a lot more than a lonely Army brat hiding behind those emerald eyes. There's spunk and wit and determination. And a lot of attitude, but even though it irked me when I dragged her out of the ocean, now I kind of like it.

I'm still staring after the girl when Lucy bounces down the stairs, her smooth black hair pulled into matching pigtails like a schoolgirl. "Ross? What are you doing here?"

I stand up and head over to one of the booths by the door where I can still see the girl who's traveled everywhere I want to go. "I've been really hungry for pizza so I thought I'd stop by."

Lucy joins me, sitting across the table from me and blocking my view of the front counter. "Did you meet our new employee?"

"Yeah, I did." I don't elaborate on when we met. "She's not as bad as you made her seem."

Lucy's face flushes. "I didn't say she was bad; she just hasn't really opened up to us at all. I can tell she doesn't want to be here."

I wouldn't want to be here either if I'd been all around the world. But even though I've only ever lived here, just like the traveling girl, I wish I were elsewhere.

"So you and Ernie looked pretty cozy on the beach. The other night. When's the wedding?" I tease, needing a change in topic to get my head clear.

Lucy rolls her eyes but pink blushes across her warm olive skin. "We're not getting married. At least not now."

I arch an eyebrow at her. "But eventually? Really?"

"I...I don't know. I mean, it's complicated. I'm going to have a law internship next summer so I won't even be on the island any more, and Earnest is going to move to D.C. when he graduates in December. I just...I'm not sure how we're supposed to make it work when we're not on the island."

I frown and study Lucy's dark almond eyes. I know what she means; the island has a sort of magic to it. While the rest of the world moves on, we remain stranded in time, never changing. I know that this will eventually change, when Lucy's not here for the summer or Earnest moves to D.C. or I travel the world. Someday, the spell over the island will break and we'll all have to move on from our summers spent together, but not today. We still have one summer left.

"You guys will make it work. He lives in Pennsylvania except for during the summer and you live here and you guys have made it work despite the distance so far. Plus, I'm pretty sure Ernie would die if you broke up with him."

I wish I could give her more advice, but I know crap about love. I've never had a relationship that lasted longer than a few months and I've certainly never felt anything at all similar to what Earnest and Lucy feel for each other. They love each other, and if I'm honest with myself, sometimes I'm jealous of whatever it is they share.

"Two greasy pizzas, order up!"

I didn't even notice the traveling girl approach us, but I grin at her smirk and sing-song voice as she balances the two huge, heart attack-inducing pies in one hand. We meet eyes and I feel a thrill as she walks towards me.

With her eyes on me, however, she doesn't notice a chair sitting cockeyed from one of the tables. Her foot gets stuck in one of the rungs and she starts to topple forward. I jump out of the booth and catch her as she falls. I wrap my hands around her waist and she collides with my chest--and I can't help but laugh. My hands linger on the slender curve of her hip longer than they should, and I have to force myself to pull away from her. She laughs with me as she rights herself, but it's too late for the pizza. It's splattered all over the both of us, but lucky for the girl, her apron caught most of the spray. I wasn't quite so lucky.

"Holy crap!" she exclaims, jumping away from me and laughing at my t-shirt, completely covered in spaghetti sauce. "I'm so sorry."

She bites her lip as she says this to hold back a laugh.

"Yeah, I can tell how sorry you are." But just like her, I can't stop smiling.

"If only I could make it up to you," she says, batting her eyelashes. I know it's a farce, but for a moment I forget what she's saying and stare at her. The joke fades between us and her expression changes.

Her voice soft, she murmurs, "Why are you always saving me?"

Her smile disappears as she says this, transforming her features into a serious, wondering expression. I've only seen her cynical and rude or teasing and laughing, but this look on her face is something entirely different. Her freckles and bright eyes stand out against her pale skin and she looks at me, into me. For a moment, she knows me. I feel a rush of vulnerability.

"I think you're just trying to get me to take my shirt off again," I say, gesturing to my stained, dripping wet t-shirt.

Her wondering, open expression is replaced by something hard and cynical, her eyes half-lidded and smile cocked. For a minute, I miss the searching way she studied me like I was something interesting, something worth knowing.

"I take it you two've met?"

Lucy. To be honest, between the pizza, the fall, and the captivating look on the girl's face, I completely forgot she was there.

"Uh, yeah. We've met," I answer, grinning at the girl.

I don't want to tell Lucy anything else; I like having these secrets between us, something to tie us together.

"Wait, you two know each other?" the girl asks, pointing to me and Lucy and then resting one hand on her hip.

Lucy and I share a look. "We've known each other our entire lives," Lucy explains. "I've seen Ross in diapers."

"Ross," the girl says, tasting my name like it's a fine wine. "I should probably say it's nice to meet you or some crap like that."

"Don't bother," I respond. "We both know you weren't too fond of me when we met."

"True," she answers.

"Uh, this is Riley," Lucy says, interjecting herself in the conversation again. "She's staying here for the summer."

Riley.

"Lucky me." The girl, Riley, rolls her eyes.

"So, since you're new to the island and all, what do you think so far?" I ask, winking at her.

"I've lived in worse places."

"Hear that, Luc?" I say, elbowing Lucy. "Our island's not the worst."

"But I did live next to a trash dump for a while, so it's a low standard."

I laugh, but I watch Lucy frown next to me. Maybe Riley's sense of humor is an acquired taste--if so, I seem to have acquired it. I like her no-nonsense wit and deadpan humor.

"I should probably get you another pizza," Riley finally says, bending down to pick up the worthless cardboard pizza boxes. "And clean up the floor. Holy crap, I made a mess."

Riley disappears into the back room again, and Lucy eyes me suspiciously. "What was that all about?"

"What?" I ask, playing dumb.

"You and Riley." A smile grows across Lucy's cherub face. "You like her, don't you?"

I roll my eyes, but again I smile as I look back into the kitchen to girl with the glowing green eyes, ready wit, and restless spirit. I do like her, but more than that, I want to know more about her. Usually, within a few minutes of getting to know someone, I feel like I know everything I'll ever want to know about them. I can read most people like a book, but with Riley, I think I've only scanned the prologue. There's so much more that I haven't seen, and I realize I want to keep reading.

"She's...interesting." Fascinating, captivating, enthralling.

Lucy raises a slender eyebrow. "If I didn't know better, I'd say you were flirting with a mainlander."

"If I didn't know better, I'd say you were in love with one."

"Touche."

"Are you coming tonight?" Lucy asks, referencing our almost daily bonfires on the beach.

"I think I actually can tonight. Dad swore he'd watch the kids so I can stay past ten too."

Lucy laughs. "Aren't you getting crazy in your old age."

"Did you invite Riley?" I ask, gesturing towards the girl as she comes towards us.

"No, I didn't think she'd come," Lucy says, and I get the feeling she's already tired of Riley's devil-may-care attitude.

"Give her a chance, Luc."

Riley, her long hair pulled into a swishing ponytail, returns with two pizzas and a mop and bucket in hand. She carries two pizzas and sets them on the booth where Lucy and I were sitting and then starts to scrub the floor with the mop.

"So, uh, Riley, are you busy tonight?" Lucy asks.

Riley looks up at Lucy, leaning the handle of the mop against her hip, and rolls her eyes. "Yeah, I'm booked. Netflix waits for no man."

"Do you want to join us at the beach for a bonfire?"

Riley's eyes jump to mine. "Us?"

I shrug and smile. "It's a tradition. All the islanders, and people like you here for the summer, come down to the beach and hang out for a while. No swimming in the ocean, I promise."

Riley laughs, leaning her head back and opening her mouth wide. "Maybe I can tear myself away from Scandal. Just for one night."

"You won't regret it."

~~~~~

This chapter gave me all the happy feelings. Aren't they super precious? Thanks so much for getting Washed Up to 250 reads! I'm so glad people are enjoying this story. If you're enjoying so far, be sure to vote and leave me a comment letting me know what you think. Who's your favorite character so far and why?

~ Hannah

Lunar Tide

R iley

     Lunar tide. Noun. [loo-ner tahyd]. The part of a terrestrial tide that's due to the mutual attraction between earth and moon.

I think I've lost my mind.

I stand in front of my full-length mirror debating which pair of shorts makes my butt look better to go to a stupid bonfire with a guy I just met. This is absolutely ridiculous; I shouldn't be trying to impress Ross, a random lifeguard who never leaves this island, a guy who wants to travel but hasn't, a man who's managed to save my butt on more than one occasion. I shouldn't care what he thinks; I usually don't care what anyone thinks, but this time, I do. He looked at me like I was more than the labels slapped on me by my peers. He wasn't put off by my barbed wit and sarcastic insults. In fact, he might have even been flirting with me.

The jean shorts are definitely better. I wiggle into the shorts and pull on a dark purple tank top, refusing to check my appearance again. I look fine, or at least as good as I'm going to look.

Ross. There was something about him, a wistfulness in his eyes and a genuine sweetness to his temperament, that showed he was more than the moron who pulled me out of the ocean kicking and screaming or the guy who caught me when I tripped over a chair like an idiot. Knowing my luck, I'll probably give him something new to make fun of tonight at the bonfire.

Despite my dedication to hating this island, I realize I like the idea of joining Lucy and Ross and their friends at the bonfire, of belonging to something beyond my cold, eclectic family. I want to spend a night with Ross, his easy charm and his disguised yearning for something beyond this island.

But at the same time, I know I'm probably making a huge mistake, letting myself be drawn into this group of friends. I'm going to leave at the end of the summer and never see any of them again, and letting myself get attached will only make it harder. If I stay in my room and watch Netflix, I'll be able to leave with no tears, no pain. But if I go tonight, if I let myself spend time with Ross and Lucy and the rest of them, I know I'll leave with no regrets.

Do I choose safety or take a chance? The good thing is, I've always been good at taking risks because I know I can run away when things get hard, and this summer, I can leave it all behind when I make a mistake and mess everything up like I know I will. For some reason, though, Ross scares me. He's more dangerous than a summer flirtation or a witty friend; there's something about him that could pull me in too far, just like the riptide that almost drowned me.

Here's the thing about me and guys: I don't do relationships, I don't do hook-ups, and I don't do complicated. Basically, I avoid men at all costs because I refuse to lose myself in someone. My mom loves my dad too much, and because of that, she never stands up to him. I refuse to become someone tied down by another person, so I won't let myself feel anything beyond mild interest in a guy. As soon as my heart starts to pound too fast in my chest, I get rid of them.

But now I'm getting ready to go to a bonfire with this guy I only met a few days ago, and I know I can't let him get too close, but I also don't know if I can stop myself.

Get it together, Olson.

I slam the door shut to Lucy's and my room and glance in the mirror in the bathroom one last time--my hair is down, the chestnut color highlighted by auburn strands. Since I'm not drenched in salt-water or covered in ketchup, I figure this is a big improvement over the last few times I've seen Ross.

"Riley, are you coming?" Lucy hollers up the stairs. I sigh and thump down the stairs. "I'm here, I'm here."

Lucy's nose is two inches from her phone. "Good, I don't want to be late."

"So tell me about Earnest," I say, elbowing her as she slips her phone into her pocket.

I feel a sense of pride when her face blushes. "He's my, uh, boyfriend. Kind of."

We leave A Pizza the Action through the backdoor and walk down the sidewalk, lit by the fluorescent street lights and the headlights of a few cars. The entire island transforms under the darkness, becoming magical and ethereal without the whirl of traffic and chatter of tourists.

"How do you have a sort of boyfriend?" I ask Lucy.

"Well, I mean we're together, but I live on the island the rest of the year and he lives in Pennsylvania, so we're long distance except for the summer, and...I don't know. It's complicated."

I laugh. "I know complicated."

Lucy cocks her head and looks at me as we cross the street and head for the sand dunes. "Really?"

"Not with relationships--I don't know crap about those--but my life is one giant complication. I've never had things be simple, like they are here."

Even though the words sound like an insult, I realize how much I crave the simplicity that Lucy and the other islanders have here. They have worries, of course, but they have routine, tradition, family to lean on when they face challenges. I have my dad the Army Colonel and my mom the queen socialite? A half-finished degree from Cornell? My charming wit and wicked cynicism?

"Sometimes simplicity is overrated," Lucy grumbles.

"No, it's not," I protest. "I'd kill for...for a life like you have with your parents." A lump forms in my throats. "The three of you are happy, and I can't remember the last time I was with my parents and we were all happy about it."

"Well, maybe this summer can be simple," Lucy says, her smile dappled in the glow of the streetlights.

"Maybe so."

Maybe I need to forget about who I've always been--the loner, the Army brat, the snob, the outsider--and try to be who I wish I always could have been. Maybe I need to forget about the complications and the future and my family and I focus on the good parts of this summer--the Covingtons, the pizza shop, Lucy, and maybe even Ross.

We reach the top of the sand dune and Lucy kicks her flip flops off to walk in the sand barefoot. I follow suit, letting the cold sand slip between my toes. At night, the ocean changes into a teeming mass of greens and blacks, the crashing on the shore even louder without the muffling sounds of kids screaming and people chatting. At night, it's dangerous.

The bonfire stands out against the night like a beacon of safety, a roaring fire that has to be six feet tall. I see silhouettes outlined against the fire, perhaps fifteen or twenty people. A pang of laughter echoes through the air and I smile. I don't belong here, but for a minute, I want to.

"Earnest!" Lucy calls as a tall guy wearing a salmon polo and khakis comes towards us.

I feel like an extra on the movie set of a rom com as Earnest scoops Lucy into his arms and kisses her, one of Lucy's pigtails coming undone in the PG-13 tangle of bodies. I stand as the awkward third wheel until they decide they've kissed enough for the moment and Lucy tugs Earnest towards me by the hand.

"Earnest, this is Riley Olson. Riley, this is Earnest."

Earnest shoves his black framed glasses up his nose and shakes my hand. He looks like someone my parents would have tried to set me up with--he's clean, well-mannered, and has a certain Ivy League look with his combed-back brown hair, glasses, and khakis on the beach. He reminds me of a Ken doll that decided to go professional.

"So you're the boyfriend, huh?" I say, grinning at Lucy.

I can see her blush in the orange glow of the campfire. Earnest drops his hand from mine, palm sweaty.

"Uh, er, yes. I suppose you could say that." He sneaks a glance at Lucy and they both blush.

"Hey, look who came along."

Now I'm the one blushing--I hate that I already recognize Ross's voice, but he's made himself kind of memorable with the whole knight in shining armor thing.

"Hey, Ross!" Lucy chirps and I'm forced to acknowledge him as he joins our little circle.

His ocean eyes glow against the dark of the knight and he flashes me a knowing smile like we already share a thousand secrets.

"I'm glad you deigned to join us," Ross teases, elbowing me in the ribs.

"You should feel lucky."

"Oh, I do."

As we talk, a cool wind whisks across the ocean and I shiver, wrapping my arms around myself. Why didn't I think to bring a jacket?

Ross notices and touches my arm, gesturing towards the fire. "Come on, let's get you warmed up."

Goosebumps break out on my skin, but not from the cold. Ross's touch on my arm, gentle and undemanding, is electric. What's wrong with me? He guides me to the fire, his hand still on my arm, and I feel a sense of loss when he pulls away, gesturing to a few beach towels thrown in the sand before the fire.

Heat radiates from the bonfire in waves, distilling the chill in the air and casting a warm amber glow over the crowd of islanders. Ross sits on the towel, stretching out his legs and leaning back on his hands. I sit next to him, followed by Lucy. He doesn't touch me, but I can sense his presence beside me even when I turn away to scan the faces around the fire.

This is a side of the island I haven't seen yet, the people who make it a success. Most of the people here are in their twenties and a few roast marshmallows or cook hot dogs over the blazing fire. They have contented smiles here in the solitude of the beach with no tourists to take away from the ocean's raw beauty.

"Lucy Liu! It's about time you got here!"

I look up to see a muscular Hispanic guy with a mischievous smile standing in front of us. "Hey, Javi!" Lucy says, gesturing to me. "This is Riley, the girl working at the pizza shop this summer."

Javier, who apparently know nothing about social constraints, wedges himself between me and Lucy and sits down, forcing me to move closer to Ross so our legs and shoulders touch. Not that I'm complaining.

"Riley, huh," he says, an irrepressible grin on his face. "So you're the snob the Covingtons took in for the summer."

My face turns beet red and I debate either punching him or running away. Snob? I've known for years that's what people think of me with my loner ways, pretentious parents, and Ivy-league aspirations. Still, no one's ever called me a snob to my face, and I hate to admit it, but it stings.

"C'mon, Jav, lay off," Ross says, voice gruff.

I glare at Ross--I'm tired of him trying to take care of me. "Glad to know my reputation precedes me."

Javier raises his eyebrows and laughs. "Well, you can't be too bad if Montgomery's defending you."

"Montgomery?"

"Your friend Ross, there," Javier says, gesturing.

I don't even know his freaking last name. This whole night is a trainwreck, and I consider getting up and stalking off when Javier sticks his hand in my face.

"Javier Flores. Welcome to the island."

"Riley Olson." I shake his hand. "Unhappy to be here."

Javier shrugs. "Oh, you'll fall in love with it soon enough. We all do. That's why we keep coming back here even though we're too old for the summer lifeguarding gig."

"Speaking of lifeguarding," Lucy interrupts, turning to Earnest. "If we go swimming, swear you'll rescue me?"

"Anytime," Earnest answers.

Lucy leaps to her feet and starts to sprint towards the ocean, shrieking when Earnest runs after her and lifts her off her feet, legs flailing as they both run into the waves.

Javier, Ross, and some of the other people around the bonfire stand up as well, guys shedding their shirts and some of the girls taking off t-shirts and shorts. When Ross offers a hand to help me up, I shake my head and pull my knees to my chest.

"Nuh-uh. No way. I'm not going back in there."

"C'mon," Ross says, with a knowing grin. "You're swimming with a bunch of lifeguards. What's the worst thing that can happen?"

"Ross, you said no swimming! Liar."

"Well, no swimming without a lifeguard." Ross winks.

Javier watches us and laughs suddenly. "Oh, I get it. You're the hot girl Ross rescued from the ocean."

I debate kicking Javier in the balls and tossing him out to sea, but I don't think I've known him long enough for that. Ross has the sense to look a little embarrassed as I mouth "hot girl?" at him and he shrugs. I have to admit--I'm kind of glad he thinks I'm hot despite my best beached whale impersonation.

He offers his hand to me. "C'mon, Riley. Let's give it a shot."

I look up at Ross, prepared to refuse, but I stop when I see the softness in his eyes and the smile that tugs up one corner of his face, leaving a dimple in the corner of his cheek. I wanted a simple summer, free from the impending doom of life choices and my parents. I want simple, and maybe I want Ross. I grin back at him and take his hand, sprinting towards the ocean and pulling him in behind me.

~~~~~

A new chapter before the weekend! I hope you enjoy it and thanks for the almost 300 reads! I hope you're loving Riley and Ross's story as much as I am.

~ Hannah

Underwater

R oss

Underwater. Adjective. [uhn-der-waw-ter]. Existing or occurring underwater.

I can't keep my eyes off of Riley's wide, freckled smile and pale eyes that glow against the black of the Atlantic night. Her hand is warm and soft in mine as she tugs me after her. She takes off at a sprint and I follow her, the icy sea water splashing against our legs as we collide with the ocean and each other.

Once we're knee deep, I expect her to stop running or let go of my hand, but she does neither. She pulls me into the waves with no resemblance of fear for the ocean that almost choked the life out of her. Once I'm chest deep in the ocean and it reaches Riley's chin, she finally stops and turns to smile at me. With her pale eyes, perfect freckles, and wide smile, she's practically sucking me underwater and for a minute I struggle to say anything.

"The ocean's not so bad when you're not caught in a riptide, huh," I say, recalling her futile attempt at escaping the tide.

She glowers back at me. "Are you ever going to let me live that down?"

"Not if I can help it. It's not everyday I have to rescue someone at six in the morning."

"Apparently it's so uncommon that you told all your friends about me," she says, paddling her arms around her to stay afloat as a wave washes over me.

I fight to keep my gaze on her face and not the long legs that flutter kick beneath her. Get a grip, Ross.

"What can I say? You make an impression."

She scrunches her freckled nose. "Yeah, I love being known as the girl you had to rescue. The hot girl."

Crap. Screw Javier and his stupid big mouth. I shouldn't have told him and Ernie that I thought she was hot; I'm certain I'll never live it down.

"Don't let it get to your head," I grumble, flipping onto my back and floating on the undulating waves.

"Too late," she says, swimming beside me on her stomach and entrancing me with her eyes.

I was wrong when I said she was hot; she's more than that. She's intriguing and mysterious and beautiful. And maybe a little annoying. But still, there's something completely captivating in her reckless outlook on life.

"So you're a lifeguard, huh? That explains some things."

"Yep. I've been a lifeguard for eleven years." Her eyebrows shoot up as her dark hair floats in a halo around her. "Eleven years? Are you serious? You've known these guys for eleven years?" She gestures to Ernie and Lucy, making out in the ocean, and Javier trying to flirt with a few new lifeguards. When I nod, she continues, "I don't think I've even known anyone besides my parents for eleven years. That's crazy."

I sigh. "We have a lot of history."

"I'd love to have history," she murmurs under my breath and I wonder if she meant for me to hear her.

I don't know what it's like to not have history. This entire island is drenched in layers of memories of my mom and dad and brothers and sister and friends. On almost every block, I can share an anecdote or an experience. Everyone knows me and I know everyone. Sometimes I hate it.

"It's not all it's cracked up to be," I say, but I know I should be grateful.

Compared to Riley the nomad, my life has been idyllic and grounded, but I think I could do with a little bit of chaos.

Riley swims a little closer to me, her hair glued to the side of her face and eyes luminous. She touches my shoulder with an icy hand and her eyes close halfway.

"Hey, Ross?"

"Yeah?"

My head buzzes with the nearness of her and I blink to try to clear the fog.

"Race yah!" She squeals, shoving me underwater by the shoulders.

I power my way back to the surface and swim after her, laughing as I take huge strokes to try catch up. Her lithe form cuts through the water like a knife, and even though I insulted her swimming before, I can see the sinews of her legs and back in the crystalline glow of moonlight. She's a swimmer at heart. Still, I have eleven years of experience swimming in the ocean and at least fifty pounds on her, so I catch up in a few strokes.

I reach for her bare, slender shoulders and shove her underwater. Her shriek scares off a colony of seagulls and I laugh as she kicks and flails at me. When I let her come back to the surface, she spurts water out of her mouth and blinks back huge bubbles of water from her dark eyelashes.

"You're such a butt!" she screams, kicking me in the chest and propelling herself backwards.

With her hair pooling in the water around her and turned silver by the moonlight, I lose my train of thought and I can't come up with a retort. She looks spectral floating there and I wonder if she's even from the same world as me. Despite underlying similarities, we are so different. My life doesn't even compare to hers.

"What are you staring at?"

Crap. I'm normally not so awkward and graceless with girls as I am with this one, or at least I'm a little more subtle, but I can't help it. I'm acting like a middle schooler who just made it through puberty.

"You," I answer, stunning myself with my honesty.

"Take a picture. It lasts longer."

"Maybe I will."

Riley cranes her neck to stare at me, as surprised by me as I am by myself. "I don't get you, Ross Montgomery."

I give her a lazy smile. "There's not much to get. I'm a lifeguard and warehouse worker who's barely left the island."

"I didn't mean what you do. By that definition, I'd be a soulless college dropout without a future."

"We both sound pretty pathetic."

Riley paddles closer to shore and stands, a wave breaking against her stomach. "I meant I don't get who you are."

I don't know who I am either. I like to think that whoever I am is still out there, that I have to discover myself. For now I'm a lifeguard, an older brother, a caretaker, a friend. I'm a sideline character. Maybe if I leave, if I take the global internship, maybe then I'll figure out who I am.

"Yeah, well, it adds to the mystery," I say by way of deflection, staggering through the waves to stand by Riley.

Her shoulder blades and arms are covered in goosebumps and she wraps her arms around her chest. Almost everyone else, except for Earnest and Lucy who are caught up in their own world, has gone back to the campfire and I see a lot of people are already drifting home.

"Holy crap, you're freezing," I say, touching the small of her back and guiding her out of the water.

I can tell how cold she is when her teeth start to chatter and she doesn't bite back at me with a fiery retort.

"Did you bring a jacket?"

"It's the s-summer. I didn't think I'd n-need one."

"Well, you thought wrong." I set Riley on a beach towel a few yards from the fire. "I'll be right back."

I jog through the sand to where my jacket and phone lay next to a lounging Javier and reach for the fleece zip-up.

"Having fun, Rossy?" Javier teases, eyes glinting gold in the fire-light.

"She almost left thanks to your big mouth."

"But she didn't. She's hot, and you're lucky. Invite me to the wedding."

I kick sand at Javier and he lifts his forearms to block it, cackling like a witch on Halloween. I leave him behind and return to Riley, her chin resting on the knees clutched to her chest.

"Here, put this on," I say, unzipping my jacket and draping it over her icy, pale shoulders.

She rolls her eyes at me. "Why do you keep saving me?"

"Why do you keep needing saved?" "Good point." Riley grasps the edges of the jacket and pulls it closer around her.

My jacket dwarfs her slender frame and I watch her as she watches the fire, the reflection of the flame dancing in her glassy eyes.

"So do you still hate my island?"

She grins up at me with her soft rose lips. "Your island? Maybe not as much as I did when I first got here. You guys are like a...a family."

Family. For a few minutes, I'd forgotten about my deadbeat dad and the three kids. I'd been just another 20-something guy hanging out with a girl on the beach. But I'm not that guy; I'm somewhere between a kid who can't grow up and a man weighted down by his family.

"So tell me something," she continues. "Do you always like to play the hero or is that just with me?"

"I'm no hero," I mumble under my breath.

But in some ways, I am. At least for other people. I take care of Dad and the three kids and sometimes even Earnest and Javier. And now Riley.

"Maybe not, but you do seem to have an uncanny instinct to look after other people."

I glance at her out of the corner of my eye. I don't even know this girl, but she's psycho-analyzing me like I'm a test subject in a sick experiment. She's not really wrong though; I have this gut response to look out for others. I blame it on my parents. They didn't give me any other choice.

"Yeah, well, that's what happens when you're forced to raise three kids on your own."

She tilts her head to look at me, pulling her dripping hair over her shoulder and wringing it out. "I don't think I've ever been anyone's hero. Except for the guy I saw with a mullet the other day--I gave him some fashion advice that will save him from eternal singledom."

I snort. "That's cool, though. That you take care of them."

I can't look her in the eye, the compliment cutting straight to the quick. "Not as cool as traveling the world your whole life."

"Yeah, well, it's not all it's cracked up to be. Let's agree to disagree."
Riley stands up and shrugs off my jacket. "I guess I'll head home
now."

She glances around at the dwindling crowd, and I realize for the
first time that we're pretty much alone. Despite her nosy questions
and annoying intuition, I appreciate the way she looks past the facade
I put up. The last thing I want is for her to leave.

"Wait. Let's take a walk instead," I suggest, gesturing down the
beach. "I still have to convince you how great this island is."

Riley's lips quirk at me and she cross her arms over her chest, one
hip cocked. "Fine, but I'm pretty stubborn. I doubt you'll change my
mind."

"I've picked up on that, but I can be pretty persuasive."

She grins at me and spins away from me to walk down the beach.
"We'll see."

I can't help but smile back as I jog to catch up with her--I'd like
to change her mind more than I'd care to admit, not just about the
island, but about me.

"I have a serious question for you," she says as we put distance
between us and my friends at the campfire.

"What a surprise."

"What's your favorite dinosaur?"

The question shocks me so much that I lock up my knees and stare
at her. "Dinosaur? Seriously? Is this some weird psych test you're
conducting on me?"

She stops too and turns back to me. "No, I just honestly want to know your favorite dinosaur."

I laugh at her. "You're one of a kind, Riley Olson."

"That's not an answer."

"Triceratops."

"Much better."

~~~~~

What an adorable pair of weirdos. Thanks for reading and for the 400+ views! Please continue to vote and comment and thanks for supporting this story :)

~ Hannah

Whirlpool

R iley

Whirlpool. Noun. [hwurl-pool]. A rapidly rotating mass of water in a river or sea into which objects may be drawn, typically caused by the meeting of conflicting currents.

I can't tell if Ross likes me or if he thinks I'm a complete psycho. Granted, the dinosaur question was out of left field, but I was trying to lighten the mood. I can tell he doesn't take my inquisitory questions lightly, which I admire, but we also don't know each very well, i.e. at all, so I feel like I went too far by asking such personal questions.

But the way he was looking at me in the ocean--I could have sworn something passed between us. I'm not sure if I annoy him or challenge him or surprise him. Maybe a little of all three. I'm so glad he didn't let me leave, though. Even though it's getting later and I have a shift at the pizza shop in the morning, I don't want to leave. There's something kind of magical about tonight and I'd like to stay here in the magic for another hour or so.

Ross walks beside me, all grace and agility, his shoulders brushing mine. "So I don't get it. Why don't you like it here? You're not like me. You haven't been stranded on a literal deserted island your entire life. Most people love LBI."

"Well, I'm not most people."

"Not impressed by our white sand beaches and perfect waves?" Ross teases.

"Like I said before, it takes a lot to impress me." The wind catches my hair and tosses it in Ross's direction, so I tuck it behind my ear. "I didn't want to come here for the summer; it didn't really matter where 'here' was."

Ross tilts his head, his pale blue eyes glowing against the black night. "Where would you rather be?" I search my mind but come up blank. And I thought I was the one who asked the hard questions. I can't imagine anywhere I'd like to be right now except maybe home, but I don't even have a home.

"That's a-a really good question."

How can I be discontent with my life when I can't imagine any place I'd rather be? I want to be independent of my parents and on my own, but not alone. I want the freedom to pursue my nonexistent dreams but the security that comes from belonging. Are they mutually exclusive? I wouldn't know. I've never had either.

"But it doesn't matter," I say, deflecting the question. "I'm stuck here."

"So you might as well make the most of it."

"Are you always such an optimist?" "I'd call myself a realist. You can't do anything about the fact that you're here, so why be miserable?"

I roll my eyes. "Well, I work at a pizza shop all the time, I almost drowned in the ocean, there a thousand tourists with screaming kids, I don't know anyone--"

"That's not true," he interrupts. "You know me."

I scrunch up my nose. "I really don't. I didn't even know your last name until an hour ago."

He tilts his head to look at me. "There's more than one way to know a person."

With electricity buzzing in my ears, I realize we've come to a stop in the middle of the beach with no one else in sight. Wind catches in Ross's hair, sending a blonde curl dancing across his tanned forehead. I think I know what he means. I couldn't tell you Ross's favorite color or the name of his dad, but I've learned things more meaningful than empty facts. He has a restless soul that longs to escape, yet he remains tied to this island.

There may be more than one way to know a person, but I'm certain I know Ross.

A sliver of fear slices through me. I'm getting too close to this charming boy with the kind eyes that look towards lofty dreams. I turn away from him suddenly and keep walking, sand spraying my legs.

Ross catches up with me. "So you'll give the island a chance?" My gaze jerks to him. "I never said that."

"C'mon, Riley. What could possible go wrong?"

"Oh, I don't know. I could drown. Catch hypothermia. Spray ketchup all over myself."

"Think about it this way: How much worse can your summer get?"

Despite my best efforts, I feel a smile tugging at the corner of my lips. He does have a point. I don't hate the island half as much as I pretend and there's no point looking forward to an empty future.

"I mean, it could probably get worst, but I don't want to be pessimistic."

"That's the spirit."

We walk in silence as we go, and I can't help but keep looking at Ross with his deep dimples, blue eyes, and long lashes. Even though he seems relaxed, there's something beneath his cool facade that I can't quite figure out. Why is a twenty-something guy with his wit and looks stranded on a tiny island working in a warehouse and as a lifeguard? What sorrow ties him to the island?

"We should probably head back soon," Ross says, interrupting the peace of the night.

Do we have to? There must be something wrong with me because I'm choosing socialization over sleep. Nothing ever comes before sleep--except, apparently, Ross Montgomery.

"Holy crap." Ross checks his phone. "It's almost one in the morning."

I grin at him. "Time flies when you're having fun."

Even though I lace the words with sarcasm, I realize I actually mean them. Against my best efforts, I'm enjoying myself.

"So I guess I'll have to start eating pizza more often if I want to see you again."

My heart beats into overdrive at the words--he wants to see me again.

"If? I figured my delightful company would have charmed the pants off you by now."

By the time I've thought through what I'm saying, it's too late. Charmed the pants off him? You wish. Ross just raises his eyebrows, a grin playing at his lips.

"Not yet."

I turn away, my face burning. I have a sinking feeling that I haven't seen the last of Ross Montgomery; in some ways, I think I've barely seen the beginning of him.

"Tell you what, since you obviously love spending time with me, we should make a trade."

It's my turn to raise my eyebrows at him. "What kind of trade?"

"I'll show you all the reasons I love the island and try to convince you to love it too. In return, you show me pictures and postcards from all the places you've been so I can live vicariously through you."

My heart swells at the thought of spending more nights like this. It's not just the charm and the jokes; it's the deep questions and soul-burning looks traded through the darkness. These moments under the moon-lit sky intoxicate me and transform me into someone I don't even recognize. Someone curious and alive and maybe even happy.

"What do I get out of this?" I cross my arms over my chest.

"The delight of my company." I roll my eyes. "Seriously though, this island is more than it seems. Let me prove it to you."

As I stare up at him, I find that I couldn't care less about the stupid island. Ross himself is more than he seems, and he's what I really want to explore.

"Why do you care so much about where I've traveled?"

"I've never been anywhere, but you've been everywhere. You've lived the life I've always wanted." I picture the album in my luggage full of postcards from the places I've been. I never saw much value it as any more than a sentimental keepsake, but in Ross's eyes, it's a treasure.

"You've always wanted to move eighteen times and be abandoned by your parents on a desert island?" I say, cynicism barbing my words.

I'd trade places with Ross in a minute. At least he has a family, a real family. At least he has friends and history and memories tied to a home. My memories are scattered across the globe, disassociated snapshots of where I've been. Nothing in my past tells me who I am or who I will be. I'm adrift at sea, flotsam and jetsam left to the will of the waves.

"Riley, I don't just want to know where you've been. I--I want to see it all through your eyes."

I shiver, but not from the cold. No one's ever wanted to understand my point of view before. My guidance counselors couldn't figure out why I was so bright but so disconnected from everything. My parents didn't understand why I threw fits when they were late to pick me up or I came home to a locked house. My friends never cared why

I started crying every time they were busy with their families. If I'm honest, no one has ever taken more than a passing interest in me. I'm a nothing, a ghost on the outside of society, the sort of person you see without seeing.

"Why don't you go and see the world yourself?"

"And miss out on your colorful commentary? Never." I want to ask Ross why he hasn't left the island, but I remind myself I've only known him for three days. You have all summer to find out.

"Fine, it's a deal."

"Do you work Wednesday morning?" he asks.

"At ten."

"Perfect. I start at nine. Meet me here at seven."

"What are we going to do?" I ask, itching with curiosity to know where he'll take me.

I wonder if he'll invite Javier and Lucy and the others, but I secretly hope he doesn't. I don't know them yet, not the way something inside of me knows Ross.

"You're terrible at surprises, aren't you?"

"The last time I got a surprise, my parents told me I was living here for the summer."

"By the end of this summer, that'll be the best surprise you were ever given."

Ross and I reach the stairs that lead back to the rest of the island, and I realize I have to come back to reality, full of pizza sauce, too much dough, and filthy dishes. I like the reality of the wind and the waves and Ross so much better.

Instead of walking up the stairs, Ross stops and stares at me, his eyes intent and warm against the black, starlit night. There's a kindness to his face with the deep, permanent dimples and laugh lines at the corners of his eyes. In some ways, he looks so much older than his twenty-something years.

"What do you see when you look at the ocean?" Ross asks suddenly, looking over my head to gaze at the sea.

"What sort of question is that?"

"It's no weirder than you asking me my favorite dinosaur."

"Fine." I close my eyes for a moment and picture the expanse of the sea, frothing and foaming with the undulating tides. "I see--I see mystery. A deep, impenetrable enigma with the power to destroy someone in a moment. It's...it's desolate and powerful and danger-ous."

I open my eyes again and Ross draws closer to me, eyes thoughtful as he nods. "All I see when I look at the ocean is--is something larger than myself. A reminder of how little I am, how insignificant and unimportant. That I have only a few short years to try to make something out of my life, to do something or be someone worth remembering."

His words reflect the difference between our outlooks on life. Where I harbor fear, Ross's idealism and curiosity and bravery grow. I see danger; he sees opportunity. But I see timidity in Ross's answer too; while I'm afraid of being destroyed, he's afraid of his own in-significance. In all reality, compared to the ocean, we're nothing more than two grains of sand.

A gust of wind rips between us, drawing strands of my hair into Ross's face. He reaches for the wind-whisked tendril and tucks it behind my ear, his touch burning a trail behind it. His hand lingers on my face, framing my chin.

When I try to speak, my voice trembles. "Wh-what do you want to do that's worth remembering?"

"I want to live," he murmurs under his breath.

And I realize this is what we have in common; we've walked through our lives as shells, never actually living, and for some reason, being around him makes me want to wake up from this sleepwalk.

"I want to live too," I whisper.

And so I do. I lean up and kiss Ross, our lips first brushing and then savoring and then devouring each other like we've become each other's oceans. There's a tidal wave in my chest that threatens to overflow, pushing me closer and closer to Ross as he swallows me whole.

~~~~~

Surprise! What'd you think of this chapter and what's happening between Riley and Ross? What about their trade to share the island and the world with each other? Thanks for reading!

~ Hannah

Eddy

R^{oss}

Eddy. Noun. [ed-ee]. A current at variance with the main current in a stream of liquid or gas, especially one having a rotary or whirling motion.

I still can't believe Riley kissed me.

Granted, she ran back to the pizza shop right afterwards without so much as a goodbye, but still. She kissed me. Or maybe I kissed her. Honestly, I don't know; there was a gravitational pull between us that drew us into each other against our will. We were intoxicated by the heady aura of the black sky and crashing waves. I shouldn't have been surprised that her kiss matched her spirit: wild, hungry, searching.

Now, in the light of day, I wonder if things will be different. I wonder if she'll even show up to our psuedo-date tomorrow morning. It's taken everything in me to keep from jogging over to the pizza shop to say hi like some sort of clingy stalker, but there's something about her that draws me in like a siren from the sea. I don't just want her; I want more of her, the same more I want from the entire world. Riley has become synonymous with my desire for escape and exploration.

I lean against the wooden back of the lifeguard chair and stretch my legs out, casting my gaze between the two black and white checkered flags that mark the swimming area. With the official start of summer, the beach swarms with sunscreen-slathered tourists and shrieking children and I have a headache from just sitting here. Even the distraction of Riley just makes me anxious to leave the beach so tomorrow comes sooner.

"Hey, Ross."

I lean forward and look down at the beach below me to find Earnest staring up in a t-shirt and swim trunks. "Please tell me my shift's over and you're here to relieve me."

"You still have ten minutes."

I groan. I remember when this job used to be fun. Teenage me had hopes of Baywatch-esque rescues of hot girls in bikinis, but I pretty much only go after screaming kids in floaties or guys who drank too much and lost all muscular control.

"Mind if I join you?" Ernie asks and I scooch over to make room for him.

He sighs and leans back next to me, eyes skimming the ocean. "So you were out late the other night."

I groan. I expected friendly ribbing from Javier, but not from Earnest. Not after he ditched us summer after summer to spend time with Lucy.

Ernie laughs. "I'm just saying. You guys were still on the beach when Lucy and I went home, and we're usually the last ones."

"Oh, screw off, Ernie. Not all of us are destined for serial monogamy like you and Lucy."

This just makes him laugh harder. "I didn't expect to see you coupling off at the beginning of the summer."

"I'm not coupling off."

"That's not what I heard. I heard you're taking the new girl on a date in the morning."

I glare at Earnest. This is what happens when the girl you're into lives with your best friend's girlfriend. There are no secrets on this island.

"That sounds an awful lot like a date."

I check my watch. "Six minutes. Give me one good reason why I shouldn't shove you off the chair."

"Seriously, Ross, what's going on?"

I can't look into Earnest's eyes. What's going on? I want to get off this island and go travel the world for a year. I want to talk to a girl I just met even more than I want to make out with her. I hate so much about my life right now and this rich girl with pain hiding behind her emerald eyes is just about the best thing to happen to me in a long time.

But I can't tell him any of that. We're friends, but Javier and Earnest don't know what life is like here after the end of the summer. They go back to their own lives, and I stay here, loading crap into the backs of semis and babysitting. We're friends, but I'm not about to spill my deepest thoughts to him. Not like I did with Riley.

I just shrug my shoulders. "She's hot. What can I say?"

It's more than that; I can't explain it, but it's so much more.

"Whatever, man. I was just curious. What are you guys doing tomorrow?"

I push off the back of the chair and jump into the sand, knees bending on impact. "And my shift's over." I grin up at Ernie. "Have fun."

As I walk home, I can't get my mind off of her. The kiss was phenomenal, earth-shattering, intoxicating, but I've only known the girl for a week. What was I thinking? But I know the truth; I wasn't. I was feeling, and that's even more dangerous. So we kissed. Will she even show up tomorrow for our first date or whatever it is?

I shake my head as I walk. I need to get her out of my head; none of this will last beyond the summer, so I'm stupid to let her take up so much of my mind. The problem is, the alternative distraction is much less pleasant. Dad. Yesterday, he got drunk before the bike shop even closed and I had to leave my afternoon shift to come home and watch the kids.

He didn't used to be like this even after Mom. As I got older and was able to take more responsibility, he slowly lost himself to drinking. At first it was just on an odd weekend or two and then once a week, but now it's almost every night. I've tolerated it because who am I to fault him for trying to deal with all the crap that happened?

We're all upset, but the way he handles it punishes not only himself but all four of his kids as well.

And it's been years, almost five years. I understand that the grief doesn't ever really go away, but at some point, he has to take responsibility and be a dad. At least I hope he does. I've been waiting for him to get his act together for years, but if I actually take the global internship and leave...I can't leave the kids with him the way he is now.

I pull the door open to the house, the screen banging across the frame as it slams behind me. I can hear Mason screaming and he zooms past me, an old toy fighter jet in one hand that I played with when I was his age. I slide my flip flops off and head into the living room where Ivy sits on the floor, combing her Barbie's hair and talking to herself. Dad is 'watching' her from where he lies on the couch, a beer in one hand and the remote in the other.

"Rossy!" Ivy cries, dropping the toys and throwing her arms around me. "You're home! Will you play Barbies with me?"

I grin down at the redheaded little girl and her face full of freckles. "Sure. Go find me a Ken doll to play with."

She scampers down the hallway to oblige and I walk over to the TV and hit the power button.

Dad curses at me. "I was watching that!"

"We need to talk."

Dad rolls his eyes, wiping a greasy hand on his stained t-shirt and forcing himself into a sitting position with a groan. He wasn't always like this, with a beer belly and no interest in anything. I don't remember him if ever being a great dad, but he used to come to my soccer games and help Sammy with his science projects. He at least tried.

"About what, exactly?" he says, taking a swig from the half-empty beer bottle.

"You. This. What if I weren't here? What would you do with the kids?"

Dad rolls his eyes and leans back against the faded teal couch cushion. "Ross, we talked about thi-"

"No, we didn't!" I start to pace in front of the TV, running a hand through my hair. "All you ever say is that we need to work together and take care of the kids, but I'm 24, Dad. Twenty four. I can't live here for the rest of my life, but I can't leave as long as you're lazy and don't give a crap about your family."

Dad's dark eyebrows gather together and he stands up slowly. "So that's what you really think of me, huh? That I'm some drunk loser, a good for nothing?"

"Well, if the shoe fits."

Rage races through my bloodstream and I step closer until we're nose to nose. I'm taller and stronger than him thanks to years at the warehouse, but I can tell Dad would rather beat me to a pulp right now than continue this conversation.

"So you're gonna run off and leave us and you expect me to do all the work?"

"I'm not their father!" I yell back. "You know I'd do anything for them, but I'm not their dad, and I want more out of my life than this." Dad's face pales and I wonder if I've finally gotten through to him. "I want you to actually care about Mason's baseball team or Ivy's spelling bee. I want you to take some responsibility."

"You want a dad, is that it? Someone to take care of you?" He steps closer to me, raising a leering finger in my face. "Well guess what, Ross. Life isn't all rainbows and unicorns and sometimes we have to do things we don't want to do."

"So you can sit around all day and drink while I work full-time and take care of three kids? That's what the rest of my life looks like?"

My head starts to buzz and I squeeze my eyes shut. I'm trapped. I'm freaking trapped. Dad's never going to change, and I'm never going to leave this island.

Dad picks up his beer from the scarred coffee table. "Stop being such an idealist, Ross. Life's never going to get better without her."

He lumbers out of the room and I sink to the couch, my face in my hands. There's absolutely nothing I can do to get away from this life fate has made for me. I need to take the Global Internship letter, rip it up, and toss it into the ocean; instead, I think about it all the time. The opportunity haunts me, but reality prevents me from pursuing it.

"Ross?"

I hear Ivy's soft voice and I curse myself. She heard me and Dad. Mason is too young and Sammy too disconnected from reality to pick up on the tension between Dad and me, but Ivy knows something isn't right.

I stand up and go to the stairwell where I see her standing with her arms around Mason who softly sobs into her chest.

"Mase, what's wrong?" I say, running towards him and kneeling on the wooden step.

He turns his freckled face towards me, round cheeks wet with tears. "Are you leaving?"

I'm such an idiot.

I reach for the little boy and he falls against my shoulder, hands balled into fists over his eyes. "Mason, I'd never leave you unless there was someone who could take even better care of you. I swear."

Ivy trembles behind him and I reach for her hand, pulling her towards me. Tears burst into my eyes as I hold the two kids close, wishing I had more of myself to give them. How could I be so selfish to think about leaving them? The three of us huddle on the stairs, all broken by our parents with nothing to do but cling to each other.

And even though staying on the island to take care of the three kids sometimes feels a prison sentence, I also know I'd never leave them without someone to take care of them. They are my prison and my purpose. They're the reason that I got back on my feet and kept living after Mom, and even if I have to give up everything I have and work at a warehouse for the rest of my life, I will if it means they're happy.

Beach Break

R iley

Beach break. Noun. [beech breyk]. A wave that breaks over a sandy seabed.

I ease myself from underneath the cool seashell sheet draped over me and wince as my bare feet hit the cold floor and it creaks beneath my weight. I glance up at the bunk above me and hear Lucy moan in her sleep, rolling over.

"Ernie," she groans. "Let's have a wittle baby soon. Pwease?"

She flips over again, one leg hanging over the edge of the bunkbed, but her pillow muffles the rest of the sleeptalk. I grin wickedly up at her. I should have been recording. Lucy talks more in her sleep than anyone I know, and it's always hilarious. Yesterday, she kept asking her mom why she was on a double date in Cracker Barrel. I don't know if she ever got an answer, but I was craving biscuits and gravy for the rest of the day.

I kneel in front of the bed and reach beneath the dark stained board for a square shoe box that I take with me everywhere I go. I made it in fourth grade in Miss Gornicky's class when we were studying world geography. We taped a world map to the lid and then decorated the sides of the shoe box with fun travel stickers--binoculars, globes, hiking boots. I probably should have thrown the box out years ago, but instead it has become a repository for all of my postcards and trinkets from my travel.

And now I need to find something to show Ross. I pick the box up and scamper out of Lucy's and my bedroom into the empty hallway. I can hear Ronald's snores from the Covingtons' bedroom and I smile to myself, grateful for this little moment of peace before everyone else wakes up. I sit cross-legged on the floor and lean against the wall with the box on my lap.

As I pull off the lid and sift through the box, I'm hit with a wave of nostalgia. There's a picture of Mom pretending to hold up the leaning tower of Pisa. A postcard from Mount Rushmore. A piece of rock I found near Stonehenge. A magnet that says, "I got kissed by a sea lion at the San Diego Zoo!" Just a note: Being kissed by a sea lion is not as fun as it sounds. Stinky slobber galore. I grin as I sort through the contents of the shoe boxes.

So maybe my life hasn't been all bad. I mean, compared to Ross, I've seen so much of the world. I've traveled to other countries, lived in other cultures, and met hundreds of people I never would have known if I'd grown up in small town USA like I always dreamed. Granted, my dad worked during most of our trips and I grew up in army barracks all across the U.S., but still. I pick up a picture of the three of us, Mom, Dad and me, standing in front of Old Faithful in Yellowstone National Park. We're dysfunctional, but we're still a family, more or less.

"Is everything alright, honey?"

I drop the picture back into the box and whirl my head around to see Merry Gene peaking out of her bedroom in matching seagull pajamas and a pair of hot pink slippers. I drop the picture back into the box and try to cover it with my arms. Subtle, Riley. Real subtle.

"Uh, yeah, I'm great. Just dandy."

Merry Gene shuffles out the door, closing it shut behind her, and sits on the floor across from me, curlers in her honey blonde hair. "Whatcha got there?" "It's just some, uh, souvenirs and stuff," I say, reluctantly removing my arms so she can peer into the box.

"Oh, isn't this just precious!"

She picks up the picture of the three of us at Yellowstone, taken when I was in first or second grade with two pigtails poking out of the sides of my heads.

"Gene and Bri look so young and happy here," she says, pointing to my parents' smiling faces.

"You'd be surprised what time can do."

I can't remember the last time my dad smiled, especially concerning me. His mouth is set in a permanent frown, set off by a salt and pepper mustache. The man in this picture doesn't even look like my dad, smiling with his arm around Mom.

Merry Gene sighs and stares down at the picture, eyes glazed. "They were so in love that summer we spent here together."

I furrow my eyebrows. Something must have changed between then and now--oh wait, I know what. Me. I came along and ruined everything.

"Well, a lot changes in twenty years."

"They look happy in this picture too, here with you," Merry Gene says, gesturing to the photo again.

A blush creeps up my face. I know my parents love me--they're parents, it's in the job description--but they've never shown the same kind of affection and adoration I've seen from my friends' and classmates' parents. There's always been something missing between the three of us, but in this picture, she's right. We almost look happy.

I pull the picture from her hands and stuff it back in the box, cramming the lid on. "Yeah, well, that's in the past. I just needed to grab something out of here for a friend."

"You're spending some time with the oldest Montgomery boy this morning, right?"

I start to turn as red as I was when I sprayed ketchup all over my face. Why do I feel like I've been caught making out with the captain of the football team? You're an adult, Olson. Act like it.

"Yeah," I say, standing up and holding the box to my chest. "You know him?"

Merry Gene chuckles, clambering to her feet with cracking joints. "He's an islander, honey. We all know each other. I know he hangs out with Lucy sometimes, such a sweet boy. He's had a hard go of it."

My ears perk up. Ross, confident, charming, easygoing Ross, has a hard life? I know he mentioned taking care of his siblings, but I figured he's just another smalltown kid who wants to make it off the island.

"What do you mean? What happened to him?"

She eyes me for a moment. "Honestly, dear, if he hasn't told you yet, then I don't think I should. It's none of my business, you know."

Curiosity itches at me and I wonder how I'll make it through the morning without inundating him with questions. I guess I shouldn't be surprised; my own past is plagued with pain and heartbreak. Maybe I'm not alone. Maybe there are lots of people like me who have struggled and suffered through life and try to pretend they're alright. The difference is that I suck at pretending.

Clutching the box to my chest, I turn away from Merry Gene. "I should, uh, get ready to head out."

Merry Gene just stands there and smiles at me. "I don't know if I've told you this recently, but I'm so glad you're here, Riley."

I stand there like a deer in the headlights for a minute, not quite sure what to do. Taking compliments has never been my strong suit.

"Really?"

"Yes. We're lucky to have you."

The words strike at something in my chest. They're happy I'm here. They want me here. I can't remember the last time anyone wanted me, and I can feel the ice wall around my heart melting just a little from Merry Gene's warm words.

"Uh, thanks. I mean, I'm glad I'm here."

And for once, I don't infuse the words with sarcasm. For once, I'm happy to be where I am right now.

I give Merry Gene a small, hesitant smile and rush back into my room. I dig through the box of trinkets and choose the rock from Stonehenge to show Ross. Somehow, I can't quite let him see my not-so-happy family yet. Just like he hasn't told me about his past, there are some parts of us that are harder to share, even with someone who seems to already know us.

I slip out of my tank top and pajama bottoms and pull on a pair of turquoise gym shorts, a lightweight t-shirt, and running shoes. Ross. Like some idiotic school girl crush, Ross hasn't left my mind since that spontaneous, magical, dangerous kiss on the beach the other night. And even though I know I should feel nervous right now, preparing for this pseudo-not-quite-date, I don't. I'm eager to see him again, to talk to him and laugh with him and hopefully make out with him again. I should be afraid that I'm jumping into the deep end way too quickly, but fear has never gotten me anything. I'm done living a shadow life; I want reality in startling color and heartbreaking clarity, whatever the cost.

I tiptoe out of the room and head out of the Covingtons' house for the beach. The sun is still rising in the east, casting a warm glow over the quiet island. I walk towards the beach, my pace and heartbeat quickening as I go. Although I would have considered this a complete impossibility two weeks ago, I'm excited for this. Not that I'll admit it to Ross, but he's turned this summer around into something pretty incredible.

I head for the entrance to the beach where the bonfire was the other night and as I crest the dune, my eyes search the horizon--not for dolphin pods or great white sharks, but for this annoyingly charming islander with perfect dimples.

As my feet sink into the sand, I see him walking towards me, wearing a pair of gym shorts and a thin t-shirt that shows off his lean biceps. Working in a warehouse may be grueling minimum-wage work, but it pays off in Ross's physique. Between that and the lifeguarding, I have no complaints.

I start to jog towards him, and now the anxiety strikes. The last time I saw him, I kissed him and ran away. What happens now? Do we hug? Shake hands? Kiss? Pretend it never happened? It's not just that I have no experience with relationships; I don't do them. I never have. Sure, I've made out with a few guys at parties or held hands with a boy for a week and called him my boyfriend, but I don't know what this actually is, and I care a lot more than I probably should.

Ross gives me a sideways grin, showing off the deep dimples in his cheeks, as the warm sun glints off of his messy blonde curls. "Hey, Riley."

I slow to a stop as we get closer, the wind tossing my hair behind me. "Uh, hey."

Ten yards. Five yards. Two yards. Holy crap, what do I do? Luckily, I don't have to flail like a fish out of water. Ross opens his arms and pulls me into a hug. I lose track of my surroundings as I lean against his chest, my hands knotted around his midsection.

"I wasn't sure if you'd show," he murmurs into my ear, his breath hot against my neck.

I lean back just enough to look into his ocean eyes. "Me, a quitter?" I laugh, thinking about all the times in my life I've deserted things that were too big, too scary for me to face. "Never."

Ross squints and stares down at me, only a few inches away. "Aren't you same the girl who dropped out of college?"

"Oh, shut up," I say, prying myself from his arms and shoving him in the chest.

He laughs and backs up a few steps, grinning at me. "You're cute when you're annoyed."

I cock an eyebrow at him. "Already showering me with compliments, huh? This is going to be a great date."

Holy crap. I just called this a date. Ross never said it was a date. In fact, calling me cute is the closest thing to any sort of interest he's shown in me. I'm the one who kissed him.

I'm one step away from having a total desperation meltdown when Ross speaks, "So it's a date, huh?"

"This was your idea."

"I know, and we're going to have a blast." He reaches out his hand and offers to me. "What do you say? Ready to go?"

I take his hand, my fingers interlocking with his.

I'm ready. But honestly, I don't think I'm ready for this at all. I don't think anything could prepare me for the adventures ahead.

Drift

Ross

Drift. Noun. [drift]. A driving movement or force.

Riley's hand is soft and cool in mine, our fingers tangled together as I tug her behind me. A date. I keep wondering what I've gotten myself into with this spunky mainlander and her sea glass eyes. But I realize I don't care. With all the crap going on at home and the internship that I know I won't be able to take, it feels right to have something in my life that's just for me.

I glance back at her and her eyes are wide, round, expressive. She looks up at me with hope beaming from those emerald depths and I wonder if this is karma, but I know I don't deserve this. Maybe I deserve a chance at a life outside of Long Beach Island, but I've never done anything to deserve someone this good. All I've ever done is wait. Wait for someone to save me. Wait for Dad to get his act together. Wait for a chance out of here. Even now, I have the chance to leave, but I can't--won't--take it. Am I really stuck or is that my fear speaking?

"C'mon," I say, forcing the insidious questions from my mind. "I'll race you."

I grin at Riley and start to run down the beach, the sand giving way under my feet as I go. She cries out in protest and kicks off her flip flops, holding them in one hand as she flails to catch up with me.

"This isn't fair! I don't even know where we're going!"

"You'll just have to follow me," I tease.

The sun beats down on my shoulders through the cotton of my t-shirt and forces me to squint as I laugh at Riley's valiant effort to catch up with me. We round the corner of the beach towards where I left our surprise for the morning and Riley catches up with me, sand flying around her as she races towards me. Before she passes me, I reach for her waist and catch her, swinging her in the air. Her legs fly in a wide arc and I laugh at her expression, angry and wild at the same time.

"What the--put me down!" she cries, landing back on the sand and shoving at my chest. Instead, my hands knot in the soft material of her t-shirt at the small of her back and I pull her closer to me. I don't care about our date or what I'm supposed to show her--I just want to be close to her and taste the same wild intoxication I did the other night on the beach.

I pull her body against mine, a grin playing at my mouth, and I see a shadow fall over her eyes as she realizes how close we are. She stops pushing against my chest and instead her fingers grab onto the material of my shirt. Heat sparks everywhere we touch, a heat that demands an all-consuming closeness. Riley leans her head back, her hair falling behind her shoulders, and cocks an eyebrow at me in challenge.

"So? What's the surprise?" she taunts.

"Oh, shut up."

I lean down and kiss her, our bodies in a tug of war as we both pull and fight at each other to get closer. Her mouth is hot against mine, and even though I falter in fear most of the time, there's no hesitancy in this kiss. For once in our lives, we both know what we want.

I pull away from her, my hands tight against her waist as our bodies brush. Riley cocks her head and grins at me--I can't keep my gaze from her lips and I fight the urge to kiss her again.

"So this is how you expected to convince me of how great the island is?" "Is it working?"

She laughs, her voice the tinkling of wind chimes sharp against the beating waves. "Maybe."

"Well, in that case, maybe you shouldn't turn around."

Her eyebrows shoot up and she spins around to see the surprise for the day--two horses wait for us, tied to an old piece of driftwood.

"We're riding horses?" "Have you ever done that before?"

She rolls her eyes. "I'm the girl who's lived eighteen different places. We were in Texas for a while and I took riding lessons."

"You're basically a pro."

"Basically."

"C'mon, let's take them for a ride."

I approach the two geldings that wait for us, one a handsome paint and the other a chestnut. Ivy's friend's parents own a stable down the island where they rent out horses to tourists, and yesterday I called them to see if I could borrow the horses in the morning before anyone was awake. They said yes, probably out of pity, but I don't even care.

I pull the paint horse's bridle from beneath the piece of driftwood and hold it as Riley prepares to mount. She slips one foot in the stirrup and grabs onto the horn, hefting herself into the saddle. I climb onto the chestnut beside her and kick the horse in the side, urging it forward into a lilting walk.

"So why is riding a horse supposed to make me love your island?" Riley asks as we ride, the soft thumping of the horses' hooves on the sand the only sound. "I can ride a horse anywhere."

"On the beach? At dawn? With a hot lifeguard?" Riley does her best to suppress a smile, her cheeks tinged pink. "Good point."

I spur my horse forward again, hands resting on the horse's bristly neck. "So, what about your end of the bargain?" "So this is a bargain? Not a date?"

"Can it be both?" I ask, grinning at her.

The sun glints off of her green eyes and her pale skin glows as white as the sand as the breeze lifts her auburn hair behind her.

"It can be whatever you want it to be," she says, the joking tone out of her voice.

"I want it to be a date."

She grins at me, teeth flashing white. "Good."

Riley shifts her hips on the horse's back and slips her hand into the waistband of her blue shorts. She pulls out a rock and I frown. This is it? This is the memento through which she'll share all of her travels and grand adventures?

She tosses it to me and I palm it, flipping my hand over to examine it. The surface is rough and porous under my skin and I would never notice the rock elsewhere.

"Am I supposed to be impressed?"

Riley grins at me like she knows something I don't. "Not yet. Want to know where I found that?"

"One of the eighteen places you lived?"

"Actually, no. England."

Hot jealousy ruptures in my chest. While she's been to multiple continents, I've never made it out of the country. Not even to Niagara Falls or Mexico. But if I took the global internship...I could go to a bunch of countries in South America, Oceania, Asia. I could travel.

"Ross? Hello?"

My gaze jerks from the stupid gray rock in my hand to Riley's face. "Uh, yeah. Sorry. You said it's from England?"

"Yeah," she say with a smug smile. "From a little place called Stonehenge."

My jaw actually drops and I stare at the rock. "This--this is from Stonehenge? You're kidding."

Even a B-student like me knows the ancient history of Stonehenge. I mentally add that to my list of places I'd like to see one day.

"Not kidding. Mom and Dad had to take me on their tenth wedding anniversary because they couldn't convince anyone to watch me. I didn't mind, though. England is incredible."

I hear the pain laced through the memory--it's funny how pain does that. It tends to destroy our best memories by reminding us of what could have been or what was but is no longer. I try not to dwell too much on the past; it just makes me nostalgic for something I'll never have again.

"That's amazing," I whisper, turning the rock over in my hand.

I squeeze the rock in my palm for the rest of the ride on the beach, but I can't find anything else to say to express the lump in my throat. Riley stirs up this wild wanderlust in me that I can barely suppress. She makes me want more out of life, revealing a desire that I've always managed to keep hidden, but I can't around her. She is so much more than my life right now.

"You're surprising, Riley Olson."

"Is that a compliment?" I give her a half smile as I slip from the back of the chestnut mare. "Definitely." It's the biggest compliment I know how to give.

In a world of redundancy and uniformity, she's unpredictable and enthralling. Compared to her, the colors of the world fade against her unerring vibrancy.

"Well, in that case, thanks."

Riley slides out of the saddle, landing in the sand with her knees bent. I take the reins and hold the two horses behind me, one of them whinnying.

"This was fu--" "Is something wrong?" she interrupts, crossing her arms over her chest. "You were really quiet all morning."

Dang it. So much for subtlety. Between watching Riley like she's the best thing on planet earth and pitying myself for being stuck on this island, I've been terrible company.

"I'm sorry. I have a lot on my mind, and being around you makes me discontent." When her eyes fly open and she flinches, I try to correct my hasty words. "You make me want more out of life. With your traveling and experiences, and just--you. I just feel stuck sometimes, you know?"

"My parents sent me to live with strangers for the summer. I get it."

Her hand reaches towards me and then falters, falling back to her side.

"I'm sorry, though. I wanted you to have fun."

"I did. I don't mind the quiet, I was just worried that, I don't know, I scared you off or something."

I chuckle under my breath. She has no idea how wrong she is.

"The opposite, actually."

Riley grins at me and takes a step closer, catching my free hand. "So our deal's still on?"

"You'll go on another date--a real date, this time--with me?"

"Are you asking?" she asks, her thumb tracing the veins that ascend my arm.

My eyes drop to where she touches me and leave a trail of goosebumps in her wake. "I'm asking."

She pulls away from me, her fingertips floating over my palm. "In that case, yes."

"Wait," I call as she turns away from me. "I still need your phone number."

"609-204-5838," she calls back to me in a singsong voice.

I repeat the number aloud, watching her lithe free form as she walks away. How can one person so effortlessly encapsulate enigma and vitality? How can one person give me the impetus I need to finally change my life?

Refraction

- -

R iley

Refraction. Noun. [ri-frak-shuhn]. The change in the direction of a wave due to a change in its medium of transmission.

"Order up!" Lucy calls through A Pizza the Action and a grubby little kid with a gut that rivals his dad's beer belly runs up to the counter to retrieve it.

He looks at the pizza like I look at a bowl of Dutch chocolate ice cream. We meet again, lover.

I turn back to the stainless steel table in the kitchen and cover the dough with a thick layer of homemade pizza sauce. That's right, I've been promoted from dishwasher to pizza assembler. I'm basically living the dream. I sprinkle mozzarella cheese on top and resist the urge to sneak a handful in my mouth. I pass the pizza to Ronald who sticks it into the oven.

"Slow day, huh?"

I turn around to see Lucy leaning against the table, her cheeks red thanks to the heat of the kitchen.

"You can say that again."

I peel the latex gloves off of my hands and toss them on the table. Tuesday mornings aren't exactly prime time for pizza sales. It's so hot in here that my apron is sticky as I strip it off and toss it in the dirty laundry. Finally. Today's my half-day off, and I have plans.

"I need some ice cream," Lucy says, untying her apron and skipping over to the refrigerator. "What do you say?"

"I never say no to ice cream," I answer. Maybe it'll help me cool down so I don't look like an over ripened tomato.

She pulls out a carton of chocolate chip cookie dough and scoops us generous bowls. I grab a couple of spoons and we sneak out the back door to sit on the steps. The sun beats down on my face and I lift my chin up to let it soak into my skin.

"So, big plans for the afternoon off?" Lucy asks, shoveling a huge spoonful into her mouth. "Hanging out with Ross again?"

I feel a smile work its way across my face. "Yeah."

We've only hung out every afternoon or morning I've had off for the past two weeks. If I'm honest, Ross has become the focal point of my summer. When I'm not spending time with him, I'm thinking about him or texting him or wishing I were making out with him. I didn't know a single person could consume someone like Ross has consumed me.

"Oh gosh, you've got it bad. You look like me after Earnest's and my first summer together."

I comb my hair so it covers my reddening face. "So, uh, you and Earnest..."

Lucy elbows me with a tinkling laugh. "Don't change the subject. Are you guys getting serious?" "What do you mean serious? We aren't even dating. I mean, we kind of are, but not really," I blabber, shutting myself up with a spoonful of ice cream. "We're not serious."

Lucy shrugs her slender shoulders, a sparkle in her dark eyes. "Of course not. You only spend like every waking moment together."

"It's just a fling."

I'm not stupid. I know summer flings don't last, so I can't expect this thing with Ross to endure past these next two months. No matter what I want, nothing about this is serious. Ross is a distraction, only a distraction, from my life that's falling apart at the seams. If it weren't for Ross, I would spend all my time complaining about being stuck on this island and trying to create a plan for my downward spiraling life. Now, I get to spend my time making out with a hot lifeguard and hanging out on the beach.

"Sure it is. Keep telling yourself that, Riles."

I glare at Lucy and consider throwing ice cream at her, but I can't let it go to waste. It's not like I even have a choice about whatever Ross and I have. He'll stay here on the island and go back to working at a warehouse and I'll go somewhere and do something that's supposed to lead to a 8-5 soul-crushing career. We can't have a future, no matter what we want.

"Yeah, well, I know what Ross and I are and what we're not. And right now, we are going on a date. I'll see you later."

I hop off of the step and stop by the kitchen to leave my bowl and spoon behind. Then I add an extra layer of deodorant, grab my travel memento of the day, and jog out the door towards the beach. Over the weekend, we swam with dolphins while the sun rose. Before that, we went crabbing on the pier. I don't even care what we do today; Ross has convinced me. This island is awesome if only because it produced him.

I jog through the crosswalk, offering a wave and a smile at the guy in the pick up truck who beeps at me, and sprint up the steps that lead over the sand dune to the beach. I skid to a stop at the top of the dune and search the beach for Ross. I don't notice the sea gulls careening across the sky or the whitecaps floating towards the beach. I only see the guy with the dirty blonde curls and white glinting smile leaning against the lifeguard stand.

Ross sees me at the same time that I see him, and he waves to me. I jog across the beach, feet sinking into the sand as I go. I dodge a few kids playing paddleball and narrowly avoid tripping over a cooler filled with disguised beer cans.

"Hey," I call out as I slow to a stop in front of him.

"Hey, Ry," he says, reaching for my hands and tugging me against him.

I grin against his lips as he pulls me to him, one hand splayed across my stomach and the other knotted in my hair.

"Hey," I whisper when his mouth separates from mine.

"Hey," he repeats, a grin climbing up one corner of his mouth and displaying the deep dimple in his cheek.

"Well, now that we've all said hello..."

I force my gaze away from Ross as he slings one arm over my shoulder. Javier stands a few feet away, arms crossed and a knowing smirk on his bronzed face.

"Hey, Javier."

"Don't act like you're happy to see me." Javier laughs, resting one hand on the life preserver strapped to his back. "I'm here to take over for Montgomery, so he's all yours."

I reach for Ross's hand where it rests on my shoulder and squeeze it. "So are you ready?" He chuckles under his breath. "Someone's eager."

"Nah, I just want to get away from Javier." I wink at Ross's best friend and Javier laughs and shakes his head, climbing onto the lifeguard chair.

"I'm a fly on the wall," he calls down. "Take your time."

"I'm ready," Ross says, tucking a stray strand of hair behind my ear. "Hang on, I have to grab something."

He searches in the shadows beneath the chair for a few minutes and emerges with a smile on his face and two snorkeling masks and flipper sets in hand.

"Snorkeling? Seriously?"

"Let me guess," he says, falling into step behind me, our arms rubbing as we walk. "You've snorkeled at the Great Barrier Reef so this can't even compare."

I can't help but grin. Am I really that much of a snob? "Yeah, but the company's better."

Ross laughs and rests his arm around my shoulders. This. This feeling of Ross's arm around me and the sun on our shoulders and the wonder of new discoveries. This is what I want home to mean. It's this sense of belonging where I am in this exact moment. This is what I've always wanted to find.

"What if we run into a poisonous jellyfish and I have to resuscitate you?"

"Are you trained in CPR and First Aid?"

"No, but I'm great at mouth-to-mouth."

Ross clutches a hand to his chest. "What a relief."

We leave the part of the beach where the tourists congregate and walk across the white sand towards the no-swim area. Pros to dating a lifeguard: we can swim wherever we want. I pull off my tank top, revealing my maroon monokini while Ross strips off his t-shirt. It takes all my willpower to keep my gaze from lingering too long on Ross's sculpted abs and defined muscles. As I reach for the button to slip off my shorts, I remember what's hidden in my back pocket.

I fish out my piece of the trade from my pocket before discarding the jean shorts in the sand. Over our last few adventures, the pieces of my past that I've shown Ross have grown more and more personal. I began by showing him generic souvenirs, but now--now I'm showing him some of myself as well as where I've been.

"So, before this gets water-stained, I thought I'd show it to you," I say, slipping the faded photograph into Ross's hand.

Ross squints as the sun hits his face, studying the picture in front of him. Dad visited Hill Air Force Base in Idaho for a few days for some meetings when I was six, and for once, Dad invited Mom and me to join him. I'd always thought of Utah as this barren red dirt state, but we we stayed in barracks right outside of Great Salt Lake.

The pictures shows Mom and I floating in the water, and I can hear my dad's deep laughter as he takes the shot. My hair spreads around me in a strawberry blonde halo and I'm trying to make the water version of a snow angel while Mom watches me, eyes adoring. We look like a happy family.

Ross regards the picture for a moment, his ocean eyes softening. "Where are you?"

"Utah, believe it or not. Great Salt Lake. It's so salty that you float if you swim in it."

He gestures at my mom, and I notice the way her auburn hair is down instead of swept up in a tight chignon. She looks young and relaxed and free, a woman I scarcely remember. "She looks like you."

I lean on Ross's shoulder and gaze at the picture. "Yeah, I guess she kind of does. Back then, before she got a stick up her butt."

Ross shoves me away with a laugh, setting the photo on top of my pile of discarded clothes. "Aren't you a sweetheart."

He tosses me the snorkeling mask and I strap it to my face, my nose pinched. Then I sit on the beach, sand wedging itself up my butt crack, and pull the rubbery flippers onto my feet. I struggle to my feet, nearly falling over from the awkward ensemble.

"How do I look?" I ask in a nasally voice, splaying one leg in the air.

"Smoking hot," Ross answers, his voice distorted so he sounds like he just sucked helium. I try to stifle my giggle. It's hard to take the compliment seriously when he sounds like a clown.

We waddle towards the water as happy as a pair of penguins, and Ross dives into the waves ahead of me, the flippers propelling him forward. I follow him and we paddle past the breaking waves to the open ocean.

"Here," Ross calls to me, motioning me deeper into the water. "Check out these red hake."

I follow him, wondering if red hake are fish or algae or some weird type of reef. I paddle towards him and see a school of long, sharp finned red fish. I squeal through my snorkel and flail backwards as one swims right beneath me. The school of fish scatters and they dart away from us and head deeper out to sea.

There's no way I'm letting one of those slimy little monsters touch me.

As I desperately try to swim away from the fish, Ross catches my arm and stops me, slipping his goggles around his neck. "Ry, what are you doing?"

"This is--those fish are creepy. Is this supposed to be fun? Because I'm not having fun."

Ross laughs at me and paddles closer, slipping his arms around my waist. "C'mon, this is fun. You can't think too much about it; just trust the water and float, and the fish won't bother you."

"Are you sure?"

"Positive. Trust me."

Ross offers me his hand and pulls me deeper out to sea.

Seamount

- -

R oss
      Seamount. Noun. [see-mount]. A mountain rising from the ocean seafloor that does not reach to the water's surface, formed from an extinct volcano.

The flier in my hand wrinkles from how tightly I'm squeezing it. I can't quite force myself down the stairs to where I hear Dad chomping on potato chips and watching Wheel of Fortune. I've told him a thousand times how he needs to get over himself and be a real father, but nothing's worked. I know he's capable of being a good father; that's what makes his transition into lethargy so much more painful. He could be a good father, but he's not.

I know he's like this because of Mom, but I'm not drowning my sorrows in a beer bottle. I'm not wasting my life and ignoring my family and wallowing in my own misery. I'm moving on with my life--or at least trying too--and for me to do that, Dad needs to get off his butt.

I shove the flier into the back pocket of my shorts and enter the living room. The shag carpet reeks of spilled beer and Dad closed all the windows so none of the afternoon sun can filter in. He doesn't even turn to look at me, his eyes dark and skin sallow beneath an untrimmed beard.

I walk to the TV and turn it off, turning to Dad. "We need to talk."

Dad runs a hand through his dark, gray-stained hair. "The last time you said that you yelled at me."

Well, at least he's not drunk. He's not slurring his words so there's at least a chance I can get him to listen to me.

I sigh and run a hand through my hair, echoing my Dad's gesture even as I try to distinguish myself from him. "I don't want to fight, Dad."

"Are you sure?" he asks while pulling himself into a sitting position with a grunt. His plaid shirt is unbuttoned, revealing a stained white v-neck undershirt. "Because you turning off my TV tells me that you do."

I release a choking laugh. "I'm tired of this, Dad. I'm so tired."

"You think I'm not? We're both working hard to put food on the table."

"I don't mean that."

For a moment, I struggle for words. Despite Dad's absenteeism, he has continued to provide for the kids and he never lost his job. But I'm not talking about the hard work or the awful hours. It's this feeling of being locked into a cage that life has put me into.

"Then what on earth are you complaining about?" "Dad, I...someday, I want to leave. I want to go out on my own and find a career that's better than this stupid warehouse job. I'm 24. I need to figure out my own path for myself."

Dad cackles in laughter, slapping his hand on the scarred coffee table. "Too good for your old man, huh?"I sure hope so. "I want to leave soon. Maybe this year."

It's the first time I've admitted this out loud. I want to take the global internship. I want to leave, and the first step to leaving is getting Dad to take responsibility for our family. Also for the first time, I'm admitting that I have my own desires outside of the demands placed on me.

Dad's back straightens and his dark eyebrows furrow. "This year? You're serious?" "Yeah. I--I've tried to tell you, but I want to leave, and I want to know that you can take care of the kids. Mrs. May will help watch them, but you--you have to step up."

"You can't leave!" he cries incredulously. "This is ridiculous."

"Dad, please..." I reach into my pocket and pull out the wrinkled paper. "I want you to give this a try. I know--I know this is because of Mom, and I want you to get better for you, not just for the kids."

I pass him the flier, a handout on grief counseling offered at the local Wesleyan church. I would recommend seeing a therapist or going to AA, but I know he would shoot those ideas down right away. But maybe, just maybe, he'll give this a chance.

"Grief counseling?" he sputters, knuckles white as they clutch the page. He looks at me, his dark eyes wide, and then back to the page.

C'mon, Dad. Just give it a chance. Indecision marks the wrinkles on his forehead, and I wonder if this will be enough. Have I pushed him too far? Not far enough.

"Don't you want to get better, Dad?"

This is the crux of the problem. If Dad wants to keep living this way, then nothing I do will ever change him. But if he actually wants to change, then maybe he has a chance. Dad sags back against the choice, cradling his head in his hands. When he speaks, his voice is hoarse and cracked and ancient.

"You don't think I've tried?"

My heart twists inside of me and pity seeps into my soul. I don't want to pity him; I want to blame him for how my life's turned out, but how can I?

"I--I don't know."

"I've tried, Ross. I have. But nothing--I can't shake her. She's with me all the time and I just don't want to feel her or see her and this is all I can do to get her out of my mind." He points to an empty beer bottle lying cockeyed on the carpet.

"Can you...can you give this a try? Maybe you need outside help. Maybe you can't do this alone."

My heart aches at the look of misery in Dad's eyes as he raises his gaze to mine--all the pain and the loss in my own soul are reflected in his expression. The difference between us is that I've forced myself to keep moving forward, letting my responsibilities and work numb the pain, while Dad shut down, booze and TV his anaesthetic.

Dad studies me for a moment, and something in his brown eyes softens. "I'll try." "You'll try," I repeat.

There's no guarantee things will get better. Life doesn't offer any promises, but there's a chance, and a chance is more than I've had for years.

The crackling of the fire entrances me and I stare at the flickering embers and leaping sparks. I rest my elbows on my knees and massage my temples, exhaustion aching through my body. As lifeguarding goes, today was a difficult day. I had to rescue a kid who was pulled out to sea, and my muscles scream from the exertion. Luckily, he lived to doggy paddle another day, but now I'm exhausted.

"Earth to Ross," Riley says, wrapping her hand around my arm and leaning onto my shoulder. "Come in, Ross."

Strands of her auburn hair brush against my face and I turn to smile at her. "Sorry. It was a long day."

I know my exhaustion has more to do with the conversation with my dad than with rescuing the kid from the ocean this afternoon. For the past few years, I've managed to demonize him and turn him into my captor, the reason I can't leave, but I think I'm just as screwed up as he is. My version of grief is just more high-functioning than his. Insidious empathy threatens my carefully conserved anger towards Dad.

"Want to-to tell me about it?" Riley asks, voice hesitant.

I turn to look at her and the green eyes that threaten to capsize me. I don't like to talk about my Dad with anyone; even though he makes me livid, I don't want others to judge him for the binge drinking and laziness. It may infuriate me, but I understand where it comes from. But Riley, she's dealt with her own crap. Before I can stop myself, I start talking.

"It's my dad." I heave a sigh, massaging my temples. "I--he doesn't do much with the kids. My brothers and sister. I tried to talk to him today."

She lifts an eyebrow. "How'd that go?"

I don't know what to say. I haven't told Riley about my mom or about just how repressed I am here. I don't know how to explain the guilt and responsibility that bind me to this island. I know she's faced her own difficulties, but I don't want her pity.

"It--well, he's going to start counseling, which is a pretty big step, I guess."

Riley watches me carefully, the typical humor gone from her face, as she runs her fingers down my arm. "Is he the reason you've never left the island?"

My entire body stiffens at her words. "I don't...let's not talk about it."

Riley's partially right, but I'm afraid to let her see the true depths of pain in my life. This is supposed to be a summer fling, and flings aren't meant to include the deepest parts of our souls. Summer flings are meant to help you forget about your life and lose yourself in another person for a few months until they leave.

"Okay, uh, sorry."

She draws away from me and I feel the absence of her touch like a bullet. Crap. Maybe I should have told her. Maybe I should have avoided this conversation all together. Now I've alienated and hurt her, the last person I want to lose.

"You shouldn't be. I'm just...tired."

Silence swells between us and I search for something to say to relieve the tension between us, but I come up short.

"So, uh--let's pretend we could go anywhere and do anything we want," Riley says and she turns to face me, legs crossed in front of her on the plaid blanket.

I turn towards her, our knees touching, and reach for hands, squeezing them in a silent apology.

"I like this fictional world."

"Where would you go first?" she asks while I pull her hands into my lap, making her scooch closer to me.

"South Africa."

Her eyebrows shoot up. "Seriously? That wasn't what I'd thought you'd say."

I shrug. "I like being unpredictable."

In truth, I want to go to Kirstenbosch in Cape Town, South Africa. It's a beautiful, world-renowned garden that my mom always dreamed of visiting. We could never afford to go and she was gone before she had the chance to see it. I want to go there and buy seeds to some of the indigenous African flowers, bring them back, and plant them on her gravestone.

Riley studies me for a moment, but before she can question my odd choice, I say, "What about you?" She tilts her head sideways, her auburn hair falling over one shoulder. "Honestly? I've always wanted to live in a yellow house with big white shutters. Growing up, we always lived in houses passed down by other Army people. They were big and empty and impersonal, and I always wanted--I don't know, a place to call my own."

I nod. "A home."

Riley ducks her chin and tucks her hair behind her ears, evading my gaze. "Yeah, I guess."

I struggle for words--she longs for the one thing I want to escape. I have a home, the type of home Riley's wanted since she was a kid, but I want to leave it.

"I think I just want someplace to come home to. Traveling is great and all, but when there's no place to return to, it makes me feel like--I don't know, a nomad. A vagrant."

An idea springs into my head and I start to speak before I can catch myself. "I have an idea."

She grins at me. "As long as it doesn't involve crabs, I'm in."

A few days ago, we went crabbing and I thought she was going to hurl when we put the raw chicken on the hooks. According to Riley, she ate duck tongue in Cambodia that was less disgusting than raw chicken meat drenched in seawater and algae.

"Spend the 4th of July with my family."

Riley snatches her hands back into her lap, straightening her slender back. "What? You're joking."

"No. You can meet my siblings and hang out with us for the day. Our house has mold and a spider infestation instead of yellow siding and white shutters, but it's a home."

What are you thinking? A few minutes ago, I was telling myself that I need to keep Riley at arm's length, and now I'm inviting her into my house?

"You want me to meet your family?" Fear and indecision linger in the depths of her pale green eyes and I wonder if I should rescind my offer so we can go back to casual conversations on the beach. But it's too late for that, and I don't want what we had. I want what we could have.

"Yeah. I mean, if you want to. You don't have--"

Riley leans towards me, taking my face in her hand, and kisses me, silencing my doubts and my fears in one searing moment. I forget about the crowd gathered around us and return the kiss, reaching for her and drawing her towards me.

Perhaps the problem isn't Riley getting too close to me; maybe it's her not getting close enough.

~~~~~

I know this chapter wasn't quite as fun and silly as some of the others, but Ross has a deeper side he doesn't like to show very often. Let me know what you think of the change in tone!

Capsize

R iley

Capsize. Verb. [kapsiz]. To overturn in the water.

"Riley, Ross is here!" Lucy calls up the stairs to the room we share.

Goosebumps break out on my arm just at the mention of his name. Today, I get to meet Ross's siblings, and from what little he's said about them, I know how close they are to his heart. Every time he mentions them, a warmth comes into his eyes and something in his face lifts. The fact that he's letting me meet them is a big deal, and even though I should be scared about how close we're getting, I don't feel fear; I'm excited.

"Coming, coming!" I holler back.

I grab a zip-up hoodie and then exchange it for a cardigan. I know his dad's a deadbeat, but I still want to look like the cool, calm, and collected girl I'm not.

"Riley!" Lucy yells again.

I finally answer her call, slamming the door shut to our room and sprinting down the narrow stairs. It's the Fourth of July, and the Covingtons gave me the entire day off from the pizza shop to spend it with Ross and his family--and Javier, who's apparently an honorary Montgomery. For one day, I have freedom from the endless revolving cycle of washing dishes and serving pizzas. I push through the door, slide past Merry Gene in the kitchen, and reach the dining room. Ross lounges against the front counter, his figure lean and cut in a pair of khaki shorts and a navy blue henley.

A smile breaks across my face as soon as I see him, and I launch myself into his arms. He reels backward, catching me with warm hands on my waist, and I can feel him grinning as I kiss him. His lips burn against mine and for a second I forget we're in the middle of a grease factory, and I lose myself in the sensation of being with him, my body melting into his.

"C'mon, guys, this is a public establishment. Show some common decency."

I jerk away from Ross to find Javier lounging in a booth next to us, a knowing smirk on his face. Ross just rolls his eyes and knots his fingers between mine, tugging me closer as I begin to draw away. His eyes catch my gaze, hazy and half lidded. His voice drops an octave and I feel the gravitation pull drawing me closer to him.

"It would be indecent if I didn't kiss her every...single...moment."

Javier stands to his feet. "Alright, we get it, casanova. You're head over heels. C'mon, let's go. Ivy's dying to meet you."

I tear my eyes away from Ross, wishing we were alone so I could let him kiss me some more. Focus, Riley. Today's about getting to know his family, not about making out with him. Then again, maybe I'll get lucky and have the best of both worlds. With that, the Hannah Montana theme song gets stuck in my head and I try to refocus on Ross and Javier.

"You ready?" Ross asks, with that teasing sideways grin that gives me goosebumps.

"I've always wanted to terrify some kiddos." At Ross's slightly concerned expression, I grin at him. "Joking. Let's go."

Ross keeps my hand in his, leading us out of the pizza shop to the sidewalk. We walk a few blocks to the Montgomerys' house under the beaming sun of early July. The humidity is palpable and I'm glad I put my hair up this morning.

"So," Javier says, lagging behind us as the obvious third wheel. "Is Papa Montgomery joining us this afternoon?"

We're planning to walk through Bay Village, the most touristy part of the island, with the three kids before grabbing some snacks and camping out on the bay for the fireworks on the mainland. Today sounds like something I conjured up while lying in my bed at night as a kid. It's a typical Fourth of July for Ross and his family, something normal families do, but something I've never done.

Ross scowls at the mention of his father, his hand tensing in mine. "No. He might come with us for the fireworks, though. We'll see."

"So I get to meet the notorious Mr. Montgomery, huh?" I say, elbowing Ross as we draw closer to his dad's bike shop and their small house.

"Don't get your hopes up," Ross mumbles. "I want you to actually enjoy today."

To be honest, I'm still pretty surprised that Ross invited me to join his family. For all his open charm and easy manners, he's more private than he seems. I'm just a girl he met on the beach--that sounds better than the random girl he rescued from the ocean. I don't really deserve the way he's welcomed me into his life and life on the island. I definitely don't deserve the privilege of meeting the kids he's practically raised.

"You guys can wait here," Ross says as he slips into the back of his house.

Javier glances at me. "Don't worry too much. Ross doesn't like too many people knowing the truth about his dad--the drinking and stuff. He's been like that for about five years and it's kind of a sore subject."

I have a lot of questions, but I know Javier's not the person to ask. And honestly, all of the crap that goes on behind the scenes with Ross's family is none of my business. I bite my lip to keep myself from pestering Javier for more information.

"Yeah, I've gathered that."

"You'll love the kids though. The whole island's practically raised them; when I'm here for the summer, they're like my little brothers and sisters too."

Javier's warm chestnut eyes soften as he gazes at the Montgomery house. Even Javier, who spends his summers away from his family, has a home here. More than that, he has people. People he loves and who love him. People he belongs to.

Suddenly, the door opens and a redheaded blur races by us, lunging towards Javier and clinging to his legs. Javier laughs and ruffles the boy's fiery hair.

"Hey, Mase!"

The little boy responds with a growl and lets go, crouching down to pick up a rock and then hurl it into the street. Javier catches his arm, keeping a second rock from hurtling towards the white Rolls Royce driving by.

Ross ambles down the stairs, two more kids following him. "So, uh, that's Mason. He's the youngest; he's five. Mase, say hi to Riley."

Mason looks up at me, his eyes the same crystal blue as Ross's. "Hi."

"This is Sammy," he says, gesturing to a boy in his early teens with round spectacles and messy hair.

"Samuel," the boy corrects with a finger in the air. "My name is Samuel."

"And this is my baby sister, Ivy." Ross's gaze softens as he looks down at the strawberry blonde girl with pale eyes and as many freckles as me.

Ivy beams at me. "So you're Riley! Ross talks about you sometimes, and Ross never talks about his girlfriends. I really wanted to meet you because Ross keeps coming home late and he says it's your fault. Is it your fault? Because you should just come here and visit us. I have a great American Girl doll collection that we could play with. It could be tons of fun."

It takes me a minute to recover from her speech. "Uh, sure."

"So you'll come over some time?"

Is that what I just agreed to? "Yeah, I'd love to. I used to play with Samantha when I was your age."

"Oh, Samantha's so cool!" Ivy exclaims, skipping closer to me. "But Felicity is my favorite. I love her dresses."

"She does have pretty dresses," I concede, and I start to smile.

"I like you," Ivy says. She turns her chin up and looks at her older brother. "Good job, Ross."

I laugh as Ross nudges her with his elbow. "Thanks, Iv. I'm glad you approve."

"Can we get ice cream?" Mason suddenly says, popping up between Ross and me. "I want chocolate. Two scoops."

"Sure," Ross says with a sigh. "But you still have to go to sleep at nine."

"Deal," Mason says. "Can we go to the fudge shop too? I want fudge."

"Fudge and ice cream? I don't think so."

Ivy tugs on my hand and I return my attention to her. She points to Javier who's talking to Sammy. "Ross is your boyfriend, right?" she asks in a stage whisper.

"Uh--sure," I stutter.

"Cool. Javier is mine," she says, gesturing to Ross's best friend. "We're getting married."

My eyebrows shoot up and I laugh. "Oh yeah?"

"Yeah. But we can double date before the wedding if you want," Ivy says, walking up to Javier.

"That sounds fun," I say in response, a ridiculous grin on my face.

We turn and start to walk towards the Village, and Ross takes my hand again, leaning towards me so our shoulders brush. "What were you and Ivy whispering about?"

"Apparently, she's marrying Javier and we're going to double date."

Ross's eyebrows arch, a dimple forming in one cheek. "Wow, that sounds like fun."

"Doesn't it, though? I have a feeling she's going to want to go to Chuck E. Cheese's."

Ross laughs, tilting his head back. "That sounds like a nightmare." He pauses and glances at me. "You're really good with her."

I flush under the compliment. "We just met, and I think I said a grand total of five words to her. She doesn't leave much space for talking."

"Yeah, but she likes you. If Javier weren't here, she'd probably be holding your hand and talking your ear off right now."

"Lucky Javier."

Mason runs past us then turns around and zigzags between us, yelling, "Zoom, zoom!" at the top of his lungs. Sammy, the oldest of the three kids, examines a snail between his fingers, and Ivy is telling Javier what their wedding's going to be like while Ross and I walk down the street hand-in-hand. Between Ivy's chatting, Mason's yelling, and the chatter of the hundreds of other tourists all around us, the street is deafening and full of life.

Something about this moment is so ordinary and everyday, but also completely new to me. I didn't grow up with other kids around me because I was an only child and I didn't have many cousins. But this organized, loud chaos is Ross's everyday laugh. Even though I know he doesn't always love it, I wish he knew how amazing his life is. I would kill for more moments like this.

"Ross, the ice cream shop!" Mason cries, jumping up and down and pointing at the stand. "Can we get some now? Please? Please?"

"Sure. Javi, can you take the kids?" Ross passes Javier a twenty. "I have to give Riley the full tourist experience."

We leave the kids behind to pester Javier, and before I know it, my window to get ice cream is gone. Ross guides me into Ron Jon's surf shop, the wall lined with surfboards and the store filled with overpriced t-shirts and cheap souvenirs.

"So this is why people come to the island, huh?" I say, gesturing to the noisy shop.

"Yep. It has nothing to do with the beaches; they just want ice cream and..." He picks up a trinket from the stand next to the door. "Flip flop keychains with their names on them."

"Oh my gosh, so cute!" I exclaim. "Do they have my name?"

"Are you serious?"

"Not at all. You should be able to recognize when I'm being sarcastic by now."

"By now? I've known you a grand total of three weeks."

The words make us both pause. Three weeks. Is that it? Is that all the longer I've lived here, all the longer I've been with Ross? We're moving too fast. I never expected us to move anywhere--for me to go anywhere with anyone--but here we are.

"C'mon. Let's, uh, look around."

The moment breaks and Ross tugs me behind him to a rack of postcards on the front counter. He starts to skim through them, and I study him for a moment. I think about all the postcards and photos I've shown him over the past few weeks from the countless places I've been. Ross's wanderlust and his devotion to his family are at odds, and I feel like I'm making the conflict worse.

"Here," he says, passing me a postcard of the beach with a few wild horses. "To add to your collection. So you don't forget us when you move for the nineteenth time."

I take the postcard in my hand and examine it as Ross offers the cashier a few quarters, and my heart rises in my throat, choking me with emotion. When you move. When you leave. The end of the summer's going to come eventually, and I'll leave everyone behind. I'll leave Ross behind to the life he longs to escape.

My voice trapped in my throat, I look up at him. "Ross, why don't you just leave? I know you want to, but...what's holding you back?"

Thermocline

- -

R oss

Thermocline. Noun. [thur-muh-klahyn]. A layer of water in which there is a rapid change in temperature with depth.

My ears buzz with the silence that surrounds us in the midst of the souvenir shop.

What's holding you back? Why don't you leave? Riley's voice echoes through my head like a worn-out record that's a little off key. These are the same questions I've asked myself for years, but Riley doesn't understand. She can't understand; she has no sense of family or belonging to keep her trapped in one place.

I step away from her, and I can almost see the wall rising between us. Despite the surplus of emotion between us, we've only known each other for a few weeks. This is too much, too fast.

My voice rusty, I murmur, "I don't want to talk about it."

Riley recoils from me, her eyes flaring with anger. "Oh, I'm sorry. I thought we talked in this relationship."

The word relationship grinds against my ears, intoxicating and terrifying at the same time. I'm not ready for this.

"But apparently not," she rages on. "All you've done since we met is complain and pine after all these places you've never been to. I just want to know why not--why haven't you done anything?"Ivy. Sammy. Mason. Didn't I tell her that I have to take care of the kids? Doesn't she know my responsibilities are here? But she's never had those kind of responsibilities. She's a single child with rich parents. Everything in her life was given to her while I've had to work for what little we have.

"You don't know what you're talking about," I growl, a metallic taste in my mouth.

"Of course I know what I'm talking about." Riley throws her arms wide and rolls her eyes. "I've wasted my entire life. I know what it's like to never go after what you want and to spend all your time wishing you were somewhere else."

"Yeah, and what are you doing about it?" I say, heat rushing through me as the crowd in the souvenir shop gives us a wide berth. "Nothing. You're not trying to change or trying to...to find what you want, a home, or a family, or whatever. You're just as bad as me. No--you're worse. You have nothing holding you down, but you still don't do anything."

"That's the problem." Riley freezes and her arms fall limp to her side. "I have nothing holding me down, but I also don't have anything to give me any direction. I don't know what I want. I never have. If

I did--" she stops and swallows. "If I knew what I wanted, I swear I would go after it."

A quiet moment rests between us and I wish I could take back my words. What's wrong with me? I never lash out at people like this, people like Riley who don't deserve it. Why does her prodding question irk me so much? As I gaze at her downcast eyes, I feel a stab of sympathy in my gut. She cares about me. Sure, she's showing it through annoying questions and a yelling match in the middle of the surf shop, but still. She cares, and all I can do is push her away.

"But you know what you want, and I don't get why you won't go after it. I--if I knew what I wanted, I swear I'd chase it until I got it. But you--you could leave here, and see what you want to see, but you don't. And I just want to know why."

For a moment, our eyes lock and she arches one eyebrow in a challenge. The words press against my lips, and for a moment, I almost tell her everything--about the internship, about my dad and the kids, about this feeling of being trapped, but I don't. And she turns and walks away. The door jingles as she slams it, and I can't force myself to move, to go after her, to stop her and tell her the truth.

The problem is, I've carried my own shackles with me for years, and I've never even let anyone see them. Riley can see there's something holding me back, but instead of feeling relief that she knows me so well, I'm ashamed by my own immobility. I do know what I want. I could do something about it. But I haven't.

What's holding you back?

Whatever it is, it's the same thing that's keeping me from running after Riley and apologizing for being such a stubborn idiot. I watch her through the shop window, walking down the stairs and away from me. Javier and Ivy try to stop her, but she brushes them off and keeps walking, and I feel part of me walking away with me.

"Bro, what's wrong with you?"

I turn around to see a heavyset Hispanic guy in a colorful Hawaiian shirt watching me through a pair of Ray-Bans.

"Excuse me?"

"You just gonna let her walk away from you like that? Have you never seen a rom com?"

Honestly, Mom used to make me watch The Proposal with her at least three times a year, so I'm familiar with what the guy's trying to say. If this were a movie, I'd run after and confess my undying love, but this isn't a movie and I'm not that brave.

"This isn't any of your business," I say with a sigh.

The man raises his eyebrows. "What's got your panties in a wad, bro?"

I close my eyes and force my simmering rage to calm--I'm not angry at him, and to be honest, I'm not even angry at Riley. I'm angry at myself, but it's a lot easier to project that on other people than to deal with the blame.

"She's hot and she likes you, man. What more can you ask for?"

He has a point. I look out the window and I can see her figure just disappearing. I should go after her.

"I can't believe I'm saying this, but you're right." I slip past the man and push through the door, ignoring the dinging bell behind me. Ivy, Javier, Mason, and Sammy stand next to the ice cream stand, but Riley's nowhere in sight. I have to apologize. Maybe I should tell her the truth--that I'm terrified of leaving, but that this summer might just be my last on the island. I want to tell her that my life is a mess and I've always let myself do nothing, but something is changing. Riley's pushing me to change, and it terrifies me.

Javier says something, but I ignore him, my heart pounding in my chest. What if she doesn't forgive me for my barbed comeback and hurtful defensiveness? What if she feels like we're going too deep too fast?

I start to jog down the sidewalk, dodging tourists and pushing past gawkers, but I can't see her anywhere. She's gone. You idiot. I curse at myself under my breath. This is my fault. I got scared, I got defensive, and I pushed away the one person who cared enough to try to understand.

"Ross, she's gone, man." I turn around to find Javier with Ivy at his side. "She looked really ticked off, and told me she was leaving. She said not to go after her."

I squeeze my hands into fists at my side. Should I go back to the pizza shop and force her to listen to my apology? A tiny rational voice in my head says that maybe this is for the best. It has only been a few weeks, and even though it feels like much longer, how stupid would I be to tell the girl I barely know the sad truth about my life?

This summer fling isn't meant to last; Riley and I both know that. It's supposed to be shallow and temporary like a tide pool at dusk, but with every confession and shared moment, we've been moving towards the deep end. The change scares me, but until today, my anticipation overpowered the fear.

Today, I let the fear win out and I screwed up. I lashed out, and I lost her.

"Rossy, have some ice cream!" I look down and see Ivy tugging on my hand, her eyes wide. "That'll make you feel better."

I ruffle her strawberry blonde hair and try to summon a smile. "I don't know that it will."

Dissipation

Riley

Dissipation. Noun. [dis-uh-pey-shuhn]. The process in which a wave generated via a weather condition loses its mechanical energy.

In the last seven days, I have brainstormed 127 ways Ross could come to an untimely demise, and I've recorded all of them in a list in my phone. My personal favorite involves tar and feathering in front of all his family and friends.

Maybe my anger is unwarranted. I mean, I've only known him a few weeks. Not even a month. Maybe I was nosy. Maybe I pushed him too far. Maybe. But because of my overwhelming rage, I've disregarded ration. I don't want to be level-headed. I don't want to think about how I should feel; I only know how I do feel.

I lean back onto the narrow bunk bed and squeeze my eyes shut, my heart still throbbing in my chest.

Angry, check. Frustrated, check. Hurt, check. I don't know if I'm more upset by the way he ignored my question or by the hurtful words he directed back at me. Until a week ago, I never thought of Ross as someone who was quick to retaliate in anger. I actually considered him thoughtful and kind. I thought he understood my dilemma, my utter purposelessness in life, but instead he exploited my greatest weakness as the object of his retribution.

Was I wrong? On one hand, until a week ago, he was funny, charming, kind, understanding. A ten minute argument in the middle of a freaking surf shop doesn't change his very essence. But what happened in there? I just--I wanted to understand what was holding him back from the future he so clearly wants. He wants to see the world, but something is stopping him.

On the other hand, I don't know what I want, but I have all the freedom in the world. Strangely enough, however, my freedom sometimes feels like it's own cage. If I can do whatever I want, then why can't I find something that I love? A career, a passion, a purpose?

Maybe Ross is jealous of my freedom just like I'm jealous of his home and family and belonging. Still, he didn't have to lash out. "You're as bad as me. No--you're worse." I want to prove him wrong, show him that I can change and I can go after what I want, but how? What options do I have in my limitless freedom? I could go back to college, but I don't know what I want to study, and even if I had some inkling about my future career, my parents won't approve unless it's stable and lucrative. I could travel, but I've already seen so much of the world. I crave connection, belonging, home, not something artificial like the army barracks I've lived in most of my life. I want to love people and be loved in return, but that's not something I can "go after."

A tiny part of me that I don't really want to listen to tells me that Ross might have been right. I'm doing nothing; I'm not even trying to find what I want, much less go after it. If I'm honest with myself, the only clear thing that I want right now is Ross despite my best efforts at hating him. But of course, the one thing I want, I'm too angry and hurt to go after.

Chasing after Ross might be a stupid goal, but I still want to prove to him that I'm not doing nothing. Fine, then. I will. I flail myself over the edge of the bed and dig beneath it in the pile of discarded junk and dirty underwear to find my white MacBook.

So what do I want out of life? I know what I don't want. I don't want some corporate job where I spend all my time crunching numbers and squashing small businesses. I don't want to join the military or work on Wall Street or become a pilot or any of the other career paths Dad has pushed me towards. I know I want stability and purpose and meaning. I want to do something that helps people.

The problem is that I have no idea where to start. I open Safari and type in "How to figure out what you want to do with your life." As if the computer somehow knows me, the first thing I see is a gif of a twenty something woman sobbing into a half-gallon of ice cream. I press a hand to my stomach when it starts to grumble. I swear I'll reward myself with ice cream after this.

One of the websites the search brings up has a list of questions to help you identify a potential career. I open it and chew on my lip while scanning the list.

What do you enjoy doing in your spare time?

Swimming? I'm pretty sure work as a professional lifeguard doesn't pay very well, and I did almost die in the ocean not that long ago. I try to think about what else I like to do with my time. Besides working in the pizza shop, I spend my time with Ross and sometimes Lucy; we talk about life and the future and our dreams and goals. I'm sure Ross would say that I like pestering people about the future and pushing them past their limits. I'm pretty sure I also can't get paid to be annoying.

Do you enjoy working with people or working alone?

My lips curl at the thought of working alone in a cubicle, hunched over my computer with a cup of lukewarm decaf coffee beside me. No way. That sounds like my nightmare, so I guess I do want to work with people although the prospect of dealing with adults who have their lives together isn't exactly appealing.

What are your strengths?

I search my mind and come up blank. Next question, please.

What are your weaknesses?

A list of possible answers fills my mind, and I keep scrolling. I'm well aware of my faults; no need for a reminder.

What are your values?

I don't know exactly what I believe about morality or philosophy or anything like that, but I do know that helping people is important to me. The fact that I haven't been close to very many people in my life actually makes me want to help others more. When I was a kid, I would have killed to have someone to listen to me and support me and guide me through everything I was feeling. Maybe then I wouldn't have locked myself in a little ice castle like freaking Elsa, keeping others away and myself in.

Bottom line, people are important and they deserve to be heard and supported. That's my value; I'm just not sure how it correlates to a career. I know I don't want to be a lawyer; even the good guys can get pulled into compromise and corruption. I don't want to be a teacher, mostly because just thinking about a classroom full of kindergarteners gives me a headache. I want to help people, but I don't know how.

Do you want structure or freedom?

I release a snorting laugh. I've had enough freedom and travel for one lifetime. While I wouldn't mind another trip to Disney World, I think I would actually like to give smalltown life a try for once. Wave to my neighbors while getting my mail from the mailbox, baking cookies and apple pies, planting flowers. I could do all the things I missed out on in the stale, temporal barracks environment.

Do you want to pursue further education?

I contemplate returning to Cornell, and I wonder if I could go back. I mostly took gen-eds while I was there and I could probably graduate in two years if I declared a major right away, but I would have to return to living on campus. For all I say about wanting to work with people, I sure sucked at having a roommate. But I hated

Cornell from the very beginning, and if I'm honest with myself, I know I didn't try to make it work.

You're seriously considering going back to college?

Fear ruptures in my chest and I'm brought back to the first week of my second semester. My roommate, Aliyah, and I had a decent first semester, and over the break, I started to contemplate a real friendship between the two of us. Maybe I would invite her to visit my family for February break, or maybe we could go to New York City for spring break. I imagined us becoming best friends and then being the maids of honor in each other's weddings and an entire ridiculous future.

I was in the sink room we shared with our next door neighbors when she came into the room, talking on the phone. I closed the door so I wouldn't disturb her, finishing the last touches on my mascara as she talked.

"Mom, it's not that I hate her, we just don't get along." I remember feeling my heart drop to the pit of my stomach. "I have tried; that's not the problem. She's just super clingy. It's like she's never had a friend before. It's so annoying."

With tears stinging my eyes, I turned on my hairdryer to drown out the rest of the conversation, but the damage was irrevocable. From that point on, I picked fights with her and shut her out, and I pretty much gave up on college. Looking back, I can see the error in my ways, but the idea of returning to a roommate fills me with this mind-numbing fear.

That pesky voice in the back of my head tells me that fear is a bad reason not to do something, but I've had enough self-actualization for one day. Maybe I'll consider going back to school, but only if I know exactly what I want to major in. Only if it's actually my choice. Mom and Dad wanted me to major in business, finance, economics, or something equally tedious, but I swear I won't go back unless it's my choice.

I slam my laptop shut. That's enough of that. I promised myself ice cream, and that's one thing I always follow through on. I head into the Covingtons' kitchen for a late night snack and dig out the remainders of a half gallon of chocolate ice cream I stashed at the bottom of the chest freezer so Lucy wouldn't find it.

It's less than half full, so I grab a spoon and dig in without further ado. This isn't because of Ross, I tell myself as I dig in. I'm not eating my feelings. I'm rewarding myself for--for a Google search. That sounds lame even to my pathetic ears.

My phone vibrates in my pocket, and when I see the name flash across the screen, I resist the urge to curse.

Ross.

No matter how much my thoughts have dwelled on him in the past few days, I don't know if I should even look at the text. I mean, I want to. After all, it's Ross. Sweet, charming, Zac-Efron-level-hot Ross. Still, he literally freaked out and closed up like a clam when I started asking him questions in the surf shop. Maybe this is all our little relationship was supposed to be: a three week summer fling between two people who are too different to be together.

But I've never been great at making the right decisions, so I open the text.

There's a partial lunar eclipse tonight. Let me show you why I like this island and why I like you.

And even though it's probably a mistake, I already know what I'm going to do. In fact, I'm halfway out the door before I even finish reading the text.

~~~~~

A little self-exploration, Riley style. Any ideas on what Riley should do with her life? Let me know in the comments!

And thank you for the over 1k views! This story has turned into much more than I imagined it would and has been such a blast to write. I've really fallen in love with Ross and Riley. Whose perspective do you prefer to read? Thanks for all your support!

Upwelling

- -

R oss

Upwelling. Noun. [uhp-wel-ing]. The vertical movement of water up to the ocean surface from the ocean floor.

I spread the checkered picnic blanket on the beach and pull out a set of brown paper bags and little white votive candles I bought at the dollar store. First, I fill the paper bags with sand so they sit upright. Then, I place a single votive candle in each bag. I slip the lighter from my pocket, only used once when I tried my first and last cigarette at the age of fifteen, and light the candles so they cast a soft glow over the blanket through the thin walls of the paper bags. Romance isn't exactly my forte, but I figure I owe Riley some grand gesture for what an idiot I was the other day. Thus, candles and the beach.

The Hawaiian shirt guy in the surf shop was right; she's hot and she likes me. What the heck was wrong with me? Why did I have to clam up and destroy this tentative, fragile thing growing between us?

Maybe I should have just let things end when Riley walked away, but the summer's only halfway over. I need more time with her.

I know I owe her more than romance, however, and more than even an apology. I owe her openness and honesty and an answer to the question that sent me into a tailspin. I have to tell her the truth about my fears and the bonds that tie me to the island. No one has ever pushed me towards this sort of vulnerability before, not the kind of vulnerability that causes an aching in your heart, that squeezes your heart and empties your breath from your lungs. This is a terrifying, enthralling, heartbreaking sort of vulnerability.

I relax onto the blanket and rest my hands behind my head as I lean back to gaze at the sky. The moon is a tight crescent from the near-eclipse which makes the stars shine all the more brightly. I inhale and exhale, letting my chest rise and fall. Just relax. I'm not telling her everything, of course. There are too many secrets for one moonlit night and a girl I just met. Maybe she'll eventually pry all of my secrets out of me like a treasure chest filled with rusty weapons rather than gold. Then again, maybe she'll fly away before she has the chance.

My phone vibrates. Finally. I texted Riley fifteen minutes ago, but still haven't heard anything back from her. I unlock it and glance at the screen; it's Javier who's on volunteer babysitting duty for the night.

"Crap."

She's not going to show up. Maybe I waited too long. Maybe I blew it. Maybe she doesn't care enough to try to make amends.

"Hey, stranger."

The dulcet tone of her voice lifts my spirits in the heartbeat it takes to turn towards her. With the sun set and magenta streaking across the sky, the glow of the crescent moon sets off Riley's silhouette and her eyes are pale and ethereal against the darkness. She gives me a half smile, plucky, undaunted, but she remains a few steps away. I hate even this short distance between us.

I scramble to my feet, nearly knocking over a candle. "You came."

"I came." Her half smile rises as she cocks an eyebrow. "What, didn't think I'd show?"

"I wouldn't have blamed you if you didn't."

"Is that an apology?"

I sigh and run my hand through my hair. "I screwed up, Ry. And I'm sorry."

"Yeah, you did," she says, her gaze slipping from mine to the roaring waves. "Maybe I pushed you too far."

"No." I take a halting step towards her. "I mean, yeah, maybe. But I want us to move forward. I didn't mean--I didn't want to end like that. Because I was being stupid and defensive." I release a sigh. This is the part I've been dreading. "You were right."

Riley raises an eyebrow, a grin playing at her lips. "I like the sound of that."

"I--I got scared."

She takes a step closer to me, releasing her arms from where they were crossed over her chest. "Yeah?"

"Yeah. I don't--it's hard for me to talk about stuff. I just don't think you'd understand."

Crap. That's not what I meant to say.

"I want to understand, though. That's why I ask so many questions. I'm not being nosy." She rolls her eyes. "Well, okay, a little nosy, but I'm trying to understand where you're coming from."

"I know. And I'm sorry I--I lashed out instead of telling you the truth."

Riley scrunches her nose. "Yeah, well, you were right. I mean, I'm kind of a hot mess. Emphasis on the hot."

I laugh, taking her hands in mine. Despite the season, her hands are cold in the waning hours of the night and I squeeze them between mine. Candlelight flickers across her face as she lifts her eyes to mine.

"So are you still scared?" she asks me.

Terrified. But I realize I'm less scared about telling her how I feel and more scared that I'll lose her if I don't. She's worth the risk of vulnerability.

"I want to leave this island," I confess. "You were right. But Ivy, Mason, Sammy, they're why I stay. My dad's a drunk and a deadbeat, and he can't take care of them, so I feel like I'm stuck here. And it's not that I don't want to spend time with the kids, but--I've never left. I didn't get to go to college or trade school or see the world or anything."

My eyes break from Riley's and I look down at our intertwined hands and then at the sand beneath us. "I got--I was tired of it all last year and I applied to this all expenses paid service internship. If you get in, you get to travel all over the world doing community serve. It was a long shot, though, and I never thought I would get in."

"But you did."

"But I did." A breath passes and Riley presses her lips together. I know she's dying to tell me to go, just like I've been screaming internally since I've found out. Go. Go. Go. "But I can't."

Riley doesn't say anything, but we both know why I can't. Despite trying to think through the question a thousand times, I've found no way around this obstacle. won't leave the kids with my deadbeat dad. I can't leave even though the opportunity I've always wanted is waiting for me.

"Ross..." Riley says, taking a step closer so she's only a hair's breadth away from me. She takes my hand in hers, racing my palm. "I know you love your siblings, but maybe it's time for you to do something for...for you. You've been waiting your whole life for this, haven't you?"

I release a long breath, scattering the strands of hair that dance across Riley's forehead. My voice low and throat scratchy, I murmur, "It's all I've ever wanted." "Then go," she urges. "I'm sure people like the Covingtons can help watch the kids, and your dad might never have the chance to change if you're always here. Plus, don't you want to set an example for them? That it's good to go after your dreams?"

"Yeah, but--"

"If you want to go, we can figure out a way. Don't hold yourself back because you're afraid."

Fear. Riley and I both struggle with fear. Fear of letting people down, fear of the unknown, fear of the future, fear of never finding what we've always sought. But her words bring me hope. Maybe we can figure out a solution. It's just nine months after all.

"Maybe."

Even admitting that going on the service trip is a possibility is a huge step. I've been telling myself for weeks that I can't go--I can't let myself go--and a surge of hope rises in me.

"So, uh, not to be narcissistic, but what was all that in your text about telling me why you liked me?" Riley asks, tilting her head and grinning up at me.

I forget all about the internship for a minute and resist the urge to kiss her senseless. It's not just that she's gorgeous and funny, but she also cares enough to push me past my boundaries. That's why I went all out with this whole big romantic gesture thing.

"Okay, this is really cheesy."

"I work at a pizza shop. I'm familiar with the idea."

I scratch my head in embarrassment and reach for my backpack, grabbing the handful of Long Beach Island postcards I purchased a few days ago.

"So, I know that the summer's going to end eventually." If only it were infinite. "I want you to remember this island, and being here, and...and me."

The strings of my heart tug at the words. Someday soon, Riley and I will end, and she'll leave this island and never come back. Someday, this will all be a distant memory, hazy from the summer glow.

"So, here," I say passing her the small stack of postcards. "Each one says something that I like about you, and each postcard picture is something I like about the island. Just so you remember." As Riley turns the first postcard over, I continue, "I want you to add these to your postcard collection so someday when you have a family of your own, you can tell them about that one crazy summer with the lifeguard who rescued you from drowning."

Riley's face transforms in the candlelight with my words, her eyes growing rounder and the corner of her mouth rising. A bittersweet image of Riley comes to my mind, sitting next to a fireplace hearth showing her kids a box of postcards and showing her kids. I second guess some of the things I wrote on those postcards for a second.

She bursts out laughing. "Are you freaking serious?"

She shows me the message on the back of the first postcard and I can feel my face heating up. Of course that would be the first one she reads.

"I like you because you're hot? Seriously? Just how shallow are you?" she says although the teasing grin on her face tells me she doesn't mind the compliment.

I snatch it out of her fingers. "Just keep reading."

As she scans through the next few postcards, much more appropriate than the first one, I start to get nervous. Did I go too far? Is all this romance too much for a summer fling? Am I the only one that wants more?

Riley drops the cards and they fall across the blanket, and then she looks up at me, her eyes bright and lids heavy with meaning.

"Too cheesy?"

"I like cheese," she says, her grin widening into a full smile.

She throws her arms around my neck and kisses me, erasing the memory of my stupid mistakes and the week of not talking and the fear that threatens to keep me from moving forward. She kisses me, and I forget about everyone else. I only belong to her.

Photic Zone

R iley

Photic Zone. Noun. [foh-tik zohn]. The depth of the water in a lake or ocean that is exposed to a great intensity of sunlight.

My e-mail inbox dings on my phone as I walk to the Montgomery family's bike rental shop, and I stop in the middle of the crosswalk to open it. An angry Subaru full of teenagers honks at me, so I scuttle off the road and stop on the sidewalk.

Subject: Career Aptitude Test Results from CareerTalks

In my post-Ross-breakup haze, I went a little crazy about my career, googling career quizzes and reading about how I'm destined to work at McDonald's for the rest of my life. Even though I've calmed down a little since Ross and I made up, his vulnerability has forced me to reconsider my own life. He has the chance to pursue his dreams, but his family is holding him back. I have the same chance, but nothing's in my way.

Thus, a career aptitude test to tell me what to do with my life.

I open the e-mail, catching my breath as I do. If this says I should be a professional dog walker, I'm giving up. Instead the e-mail gives me my top career result based on the personality and interests test I took. The result completely shocks me.

"Clinical psychologist?" I exclaim aloud.

No. Freaking. Way. Me, a psychologist? I'm too screwed up to be able to help other people figure out their lives; I can't even figure out my own. Plus, don't you have to be a doctor to be a psychologist? That's like a thousand more years of school, and there's no way I could do that. I couldn't even make it through two years at Cornell.

Still, there's something about psychology that appeals to me. I love learning about people and trying to understand their stories and backgrounds. Plus, I did say I wanted to help people, and isn't that what psychologists do? I just can't picture myself listening to some middle aged businesswoman complain about her poodle's bad case of indigestion while lying on a lime green futon.

Give it a chance, Riley. I can't afford to just shoot down this idea without even thinking about it. If I want a career, if I want a purpose, then I need to consider my options rationally, not rashly as I have in the past. It took me all of five minutes to decide to drop out of Cornell, and I'm starting to realize I might have made a mistake by making such a rash decision. I have to think like an adult.

I continue to walk, slipping my phone into my back pocket. Dr. Riley Olson, clinical psychologist. It has a good ring to it, but becoming a doctor would take at least eight more years of school. The thought makes me want to reconsider my McDonald's career.

"Hey, Ry!"

I force myself out of my career-fear-induced haze to see Ross waving at me from the front step of the Montgomery bike shop. Ivy and Mason are with him, carrying giant mesh bags full of plastic molds, buckets, and shovels.

I grin as I approach them, squinting in the sunlight. "When you said we were building sandcastles, I didn't realize we were going to create some magnificent feat of architecture."

"I-I'm a great sandcastle builder," Mason declares, slinging one of the bags over his shoulder and bending under the weight.

"You'll have to teach me your ways," I say, grinning at the five year old.

After the argument in the middle of the surf shop, Ross and I both agreed that I needed another chance to get to know his siblings. Leaving halfway through our 4th of July date wasn't exactly the impression I was going for.

Ross greets me with a kiss on the cheek, and for a second, I wish the kids would scram so I could make out with him for a second. Get a grip, Riley.

"Here, can I help you with that?" I say, offering to take the bag Ivy holds over her slender shoulder.

Ivy agrees, and I sling one bag over my shoulder while Ross takes the other, his free hand taking Mason's.

"So," Ross says to me over the heads of the two kids. "I think this is my best chance yet at proving to you how great the island is."

"The postcards weren't enough?" I tease even though I feel a blush rising to my face.

I've gone through those postcards and reread them more times than I would care to admit. The time he took to fill those out is one of the most thoughtful things anyone has ever done. In my dating experience, which is embarrassingly limited, I've been impressed when a guy texts back within fifteen minutes. The postcard gesture goes beyond what I could have even imagined. It's straight-up romantic.

"Better than building sand castles with kids? Not even close."

We share a grin over the kids' heads, and I realize how much I've come to love this tiny little island off the east coast. When I got here, I felt stranded and isolated, but now I'm realizing that had nothing to do with the island and everything to do with me. Before Ross, I kept myself safe by pushing people away with my cynicism and negativity. But here I am today, grinning like an idiot because I'm about to build a sandcastle with two nose-picking little kids.

Oh, how times have changed.

As soon as we reach the beach, Mason takes the bag from my hands and runs across the beach, shrieking at the top of his lungs. Ivy follows him a few seconds later, and the two kids throw the mesh bags on the beach and begin to furiously unpack them.

"So I, uh, did something pretty crazy the other day," I say interlacing my fingers with Ross's as we leisurely join the two kids.

"What'd you do?" Ross asks, grinning at me with those perfect, annoying dimples. "Make out with a hot lifeguard?"

"Hilarious." I pause and gather my courage. He told you about the internship; you can tell him about your career woes. "I, uh, took a career aptitude test."

"Let me guess: professional cynic," he teases me and I elbow him in the stomach.

"No, you moron." I look away from him for a minute, wriggling my toes in the sand. "A psychologist."

Out of the corner of my eye, I see Ross tilt his head and study me. My face turns red under his scrutiny; is this a terrible idea? What if I traumatize some poor person through my terrible advice?

"Wow, that actually kinda fits."

My gaze jerks to him. "Seriously? You think?"

"I mean, you're good at understanding people. It seems--sometimes, it feels like you know me better than I know myself. Sure, your methods of asking questions might need to move away from drill sergeant interrogation, but you get people. You'd be good at that."

I scrunch up my nose. "I'd have to go to school for like a thousand years."

"A thousand years? You'd be as old as a dinosaur!" Mason suddenly exclaims, leaping up from the growing pile of sand he and Ivy have accumulated.

"I know. I'd probably grow scales and start eating people too."

"Not all dinosaurs eat people," Mason returns and I roll my eyes, laughing.

"Whatever. Show me how to build that awesome sandcastle."

I toss my flip-flops into the sand and kneel between Ivy and Mason, taking a plastic shovel and a bucket in hand.

"Okay," Ivy commands, hands on the hips of her pink shorts with embroidered strawberries. "You're in charge of getting the wet sand to make the whole castle stick together."

"Aye aye, captain."

A few hours pass, and between Ross's ingenuity, Ivy's bossiness, Mason's enthusiasm, and my slave labor, we have constructed a masterpiece of a sand castle that rivals the Taj Mahal. Ross manages to build the underground tunnel Mason requests and the balcony Ivy wants while I get a rash in several unfortunate locations from sitting in the wet sand for too long.

While Ross puts the finishing touches on one of the parapets, Mason finds an old frisbee at the bottom of one of the bags and chucks it at Ross's head. He nabs it out of the air and starts to play catch with the overly energetic five year old, leaving Ivy and me to marvel at our handiwork.

I lean back in the sand, resting on my hands and heaving a sigh of contentment.

"So, are you and Ross back together now?" Ivy asks, studying me with her sharp green eyes.

"Uh, yeah. Yep. We're good now."

"Thank goodness. He was so miserable after the Fourth of July. I thought he was going to cry himself to sleep every night."

I stifle a laugh at Ivy's overly dramatic eyeroll. "I'm pretty sure he would have survived. It's...it's really cool how close you and Ross are, though. I always wanted a brother."

"You don't have one? That sounds awful. I would die without Ross." She perks up, glancing at her two brothers playing catch. "But I'm willing to share! You can have Mason if you want!"

"I think I'll pass. But no, I don't have any brothers or sisters. I always wanted a big family."

"Yeah, but big families have problems too," Ivy says, crossing her arms over her chest. "Ross has to work really hard to take care of us."

My curiosity gets the better of me, and I start to pry. "Your mom and dad don't help much?"

"Dad's a drunk. Ross doesn't want us to know, but my friend Melissa told me that's what he is. Because he drinks too much alco-co-hol."

"Ah. Do you wish your dad took care of you more?"

Ivy tilts her head, her soft curls shading her face. "Sometimes. But we have Ross. We don't need Dad."

I want to ask about their mom, the taboo topic that no one ever dares to broach, but I know that's a line I shouldn't cross with Ross's baby sister.

"Well, you're lucky to have him," I say. "But I know I would miss my dad."

Even though my father is gruff and demanding, I still know that he wants the best for me, just his idea of the best. If I needed something, he would take care of me. Our relationship may not be the best, but at least I have one. At least he's sober.

Ivy's frown deepens at my words. "He--he was different. A long time ago, when I was just a little girl. He used to smile and he didn't smell bad all the time. I miss that Dad."

My heart breaks for Ross and Ivy and Sammy and Mason. Ross is stuck forced to play the parent with his younger siblings, and Ivy, Sammy, and Mason miss out on the relationship they could have with their real father.

I'm starting to understand why Ross can't leave. I don't know if I could either in his shoes.

~~~~~

I took a career aptitude test the other day, and it did indeed tell me I should be a dog walker. If only that paid enough to live on and offered full benefits. *Sigh*

Thanks so much for reading!

Upsurge

R^{oss}

Upsurge. Noun. [up-surge]. A rapid or sudden rise or increase.

I sit on the couch, leaning forward with my elbows on my knees, and study the white door with its peeling paint and sun warped windows. An envelope rests in my hands, addressed to World Service International. It's my acceptance letter.

I blame Riley for this irrepressible discontentment. I wasn't going to accept the internship--I was going to stay here and take care of the kids until some eventual day when Dad would be able to take care of them himself. Or they graduated high school, whichever came sooner. But I'm realizing I have to take control of my own life. I don't want Mason and Ivy and Sammy to grow up believing that my current lifestyle is all there is for them, that dreams never amount to anything, that they're destined to live on this island forever. I refuse to let them follow in my footsteps.

Only one obstacle remains between me and the global service internship: Dad. When he walks through the doors, I'll know whether this dream might actually come true or whether I need to finally lay it to rest and accept my fate.

As if on cue, the front door swings open and Dad enters. I drop the envelope on the couch and rub my sweaty palms on my cotton hoodie. Dad pulls his keys from the lock, turned away from me so I can't see his expression in the pale glow of the evening moon. He wears a faded button down with a few beer stains, haphazardly tucked into a pair of jeans. It doesn't look like much, but for Dad, this is putting forth some effort.

"So, how'd it go?" I ask, standing up.

Dad jumps, dropping the keys and then bending to pick them up. "What the--I didn't know you were there. What, lying in wait for me?"

"I just want to know how it went. Did you--was it good?" Dad sighs and runs a hand through his hair, prematurely gray. "It was the first session, Ross, with me and a bunch of old people whose husbands and wives died from cancer. They're probably next."

I resist the urge to slap him. Doesn't he have any sympathy for other people who've gone through the same sort of pain? Why has this tragedy hardened instead of softened him? I don't understand.

"What'd you talk about?" I ask, grinding my teeth together to keep from lashing out at him.

He went to the grief therapy session. I have to at least give him credit for trying; maybe it'll make a difference. Maybe something will change. Dad groans, sitting back in the recliner chair across from me and staring up at the ceiling, stained by cigarette smoke. His fingers trace a tear in the leather on the arm of the couch.

"They talked about the stages of grief, like losing someone is something you can just get over."

"What stage are you in?" I ask.

I'm familiar with the stages; I researched everything I could find about grief psychology to try to help the kids and me and Dad cope with everything. The kids are as alright as they can be without a mother, but Dad has a long way to go.

Dad laughs humorlessly and grips the chair arm. "I don't know. I'm angry, I'm depressed, I'm in denial. I haven't accepted anything."

"Do you think you'll go back?" I ask, picking up the envelope and fiddling with it.

"I...I don't know, Ross. I know I should, but...they want us to think about what in our lives we want to change, and I realized I want to change everything. What I do with you kids, my job, my...my drinking."

I sit up straighter and watch him, my heart pounding a chest. He's not only admitting that there is a problem, but that he wants to change it. Maybe, after five brutal years, he'll finally attempt to change.

"You can, Dad. You can get help and you can get better."

"But what if it's too late for me, Ross? It's been five years. I should have--it shouldn't have taken this long. I've plateaued. This is it for me."

Emotion rises in my throat, choking me. I plead with him, leaning forward and resting my elbows on my knees. "No, it's not too late, Dad. I swear to you. Please, you have to get better."

"Why? Why do I have to? I don't want to move on."

His words hit me with the force of a tsunami and I lean backwards, mouth hanging open. He doesn't want to move on. It's not that the grief is so overpowering that he can't move on; it's that he doesn't want to. He doesn't want to leave her in the past.

For the first time in years, a wave of sympathy crashes over me. He and Mom were high school sweethearts who got married as soon as they turned eighteen; they barely knew a life without each other until Mom died. Even after five years, he's still not ready to say goodbye. Unbidden, Riley's face appears in my mind's eye. Will I be ready to say goodbye to her when summer ends? Will I ever be ready?

"She's gone, Dad," I say, voice rusty with meaning.

Even though it's been five years, it still surprises me how powerful the permanency of Mom's absence is. I still sometimes expect to walk into the kitchen to find her with suds up to her elbows, her blonde hair in tangled waves around her ears and Enya playing from an old cassette tape. For Dad, however, I think she's a ghost that still walks the paths of his heart, coaxing him into depression.

"I know that." He sighs and studies the worn palms of his hands.

"You don't have to forget her, Dad, but you do have to accept it. And keep going to therapy."

Dad looks up at me suddenly, cocking his head and running a hand over his unshaven face. "Is there something you're not telling me?"

I look down at the envelope growing wrinkled in my grasp. I wasn't planning on telling him the truth, not yet, but the summer is halfway over and once I mail this envelope, my choice is made. There's no use in prolonging the inevitable. I suck in a deep breath and stand up, clutching the envelope in front of me. My chest tightens as the words rush to my lips.

"Dad, I'm...I'm leaving. At the end of the summer. I'm going on a nine month service internship, all around the world. I'll be back at the beginning of next summer, and I'm going to make sure there are people to help with Sammy and Mason and Ivy. I just...I have to. I have to go."

I exhale at the end of my speech and I can't keep from looking at Dad. Even though he hasn't been a father to me for five years, I still want him to approve. I don't want him to think that I'm abandoning our family. I have to leave. I need to.

"It took you long enough," he grumbles with a laugh. "I never thought you'd leave."

Again, my jaw drops. Dad's been expecting me to leave? He hasn't done anything with the kids and he's always let me take care of everything, so I thought--

"Seriously? I've been staying here because of you. Because you can't take care of yourself, much less three kids."

Dad rolls his eyes. "You've always wanted to leave. I know that. I'll keep going to these stupid therapy sessions is that makes you feel better, but you know the islanders will make sure we're all right while you're gone."

Dad's tone of voice indicates that he's been expecting my departure, like he's known that I was going to go before I even knew.

"How did you know I wanted to leave?" I ask, falling back into the couch.

"You're not exactly subtle. You talk about traveling all the time. Just send that letter already and get out of here," he says, gesturing towards the envelope.

"You're...you're serious? About me leaving and about therapy and everything?"

Dad narrows his flinty gray eyes at me. Since he hasn't been drinking, his gaze is sharp and his observation astute. This is the man who had a great job in business before everything fell apart.

"I don't want to be the way I am, Ross. I just don't want to leave her behind, either. Maybe this...this stupid therapy therapy thing will help me figure out how to find some balance." "What about the kids?"

"You find people to watch them while I work, and maybe someone to check in on us once in awhile, and I'll do the rest."

I struggle to picture Dad doing all the household chores I do on a daily basis--washing the dishes, packing school lunches, cleaning the bathroom. But if I leave, when I leave, I have to trust that someone will take care of it. Maybe Dad won't ever change until I give him the opportunity. But he's willing, which is something he's never been before.

"I, uh--thanks."

"So send the letter already," Dad says, gesturing to the envelope in my hand. "Do I have to spell it out for you?"

I grin at him and fly out the door, racing down the driveway to the crooked red mailbox next to the main street. I glance down at the envelop one time before I stick it in the mailbox and raise the red flag.

I'm leaving Long Beach Island. I'm going to see the world.

Caught Inside

Riley

Caught inside. Adjective. [kawt in-sahyd]. A surfer who is caught inside is too far in, and the waves are breaking further out. It can be dangerous in big surf.

Despite my less than fortunate run-in with the waves the last time I went swimming, today Ross convinced me to try surfing. I have little trust in my abilities since I am an utter failure at roller skating, skiing, skateboarding, and anything else that involves something moving under my feet. Ross, the super surfer lifeguard, has met his match today.

I slip off my flip flops as soon as I hit the beach, carrying them in one hand, and I jog towards Ross's lifeguard station. The beach is crowded today even though summer is waning, which I've been trying not to think about. The end of the summer means two things. One, I have to figure out what I'm going to do with my life. Two, I have to leave the island, which means I have to leave Ross.

I'm not ready for that.

It's not like I've really known the guy all that long--less than two months, actually--but I've spent so much of my summer with him that my summer has become him. And I don't want to leave it behind, but what am I supposed to do? Ask him to come with me? Stay behind on the island with him? That's not what either of us want, and besides, that's pretty drastic for a summer fling. What did I really expect when all this started? Not this. Not these pesky feelings.

"Hey, Ry!"

I look up and catch sight of Ross, jogging towards me in a thin t-shirt and a pair of boardshorts. This looks like something out of Baywatch and I have to keep myself from staring.

"Hey," I say with a grin.

He catches up to me and kisses me, his hands framing my face and pulling my mouth to his. Well, that's one way to say hello. There's urgency and passion and heat in his kiss, and all I can think is how much I'll miss this when summer comes to a close.

"Hey," he murmurs, pulling away just enough that I can see the twinkle in his bright blue eyes.

How did I get this lucky?

And it's not just that he's a hot lifeguard who kisses me on a regular basis. I mean, that's nice and all, but it's more than that. I think I would still like him even if he was shaped like a hippopotamus and missing his two front teeth. I think that we have is beyond physical, and that's the part that terrifies me.

"So, are you ready to surf?"

"Do you remember the last time I braved the water? It didn't end so well."

Ross laughs, catching my hand in his and tugging me towards the section of the beach marked off for surfers by two yellow flags. "C'mon," he says, "I'm sure you'll be great."

I somehow doubt that. For a minute, I remember a particularly tragic sixteenth birthday party at the roller skating rink that ended with a face-to-floor collision and me wearing orthodontic headgear to prom. Not exactly my finest moment, but at least this can't be worse than that.

"I can be a pretty difficult student," I say, tugging on Ross's arm and grinning up at him.

"I taught five year olds how to surf last summer, so I'm pretty sure I can teach you," Ross says with a teasing smile.

"Hey, Ross, Riley!"

I force myself to look away with Ross--which takes me a solid ten seconds--to see Earnest waiting for us with a few surfboards next to him.

"There's my favorite surfer extraordinaire," Ross says, releasing my hand to slug Earnest in the shoulder.

"Surfer extraordinaire?" I repeat. "Wow, I feel like I'm in the presence of greatness."

Ross throws his arm around Earnest and says, "Hey, this guy has won a few east coast tournaments in his day. He's more than a pretty face."

Earnest blushes under the praise, shoving Ross's arm off of him. "Shut up already. I brought you guys a couple of longboards and leashes."

"Leashes? Like for dogs?"

Earnest looks at me like I only have half a brain. "No, for your ankle, so you don't lose your board when you fall."

Genius, Riley. My face flames with embarrassment, and Ross, great boyfriend that he is, laughs outright at me. Earnest just looks confused by my stupidity.

"Ready to get started, Ry?" Ross asks and I nod.

On cue, Ross strips off his shirt and I stare at him like a teenager going through puberty. Thank you, years of physical labor and a decade of summers in the sun, for creating this beautiful specimen of manhood.

"Riley? You ready?"

Crap. I stared for too long. "Uh, yeah. Yep."

I hastily pull off my t-shirt and linen shorts, revealing my pasty, curveless body in a faded Speedo one-piece. Sexy. Ross passes me a yellow longboard and shows me how to attach the leash to the ankle of my dominant leg, and I velcro that sucker on. After my last bout with the ocean, I may need to depend on my surfboard to be a flotation device, and that won't work if I lose it in a wave and it brains my lifeguard boyfriend, knocking him unconscious.

"Ready to give it a try?" Ross asks, and I look out at the oceans.

How the heck am I supposed to stand on a foam board on top of one of those undulating waves? Ross has severely overestimated my coordination skills.

"C'mon, Ry. It'll be fun," he says, slipping his arms around my waist from behind and kissing my temple.

I tilt my head back so I can look up at him. "Are you sure we can't just stay on the beach and make out?"

His half-lidded eyes linger on mine and then drop to my lips. "That's tempting, but no. I'm showing you reasons to love this island, and the surfing is one of them. I swear you'll have fun."

"Fine," I grumble, picking up the bulky surfboard and marching to my death.

At first, the surfing doesn't seem too hard. I lie on the board on my stomach and paddle with my hands, and it's not as awful as I thought it would be. In fact, it's a lot like swimming without half of the effort. To my right and left, Ross and Earnest start to actually surf, jumping from the position I'm in to their feet and then crouching on the board with their arms out for balance.

I watch as they ride the waves in towards the beach, balancing like it's as easy as riding a bike--which, for the record, can be harder than it looks. Ross takes a few spills on some of the bigger waves, but Earnest is a master, balancing and coasting towards the beach with little effort. He turns his surfboard halfway through the wave and I wonder for a second if he's going to do a flip--can you do flips on surfboards?

"Okay, enough laying around," Ross finally says, abandoning his surfboard on the beach to help me. "You ready to give it a try?"

"Nope."

"Great. Paddle your board out until you're in the whitewater."

I obey his directions, and he remains standing a few feet away from me. I wish he were closer, but he's smart to keep himself out of harm's way. There's no telling what's going to happen when I attempt this.

"Okay," Ross instructs, yelling over the crashing of the surf. "Now, that you're in the middle of the whitecaps, turn your board."

I clumsily paddle myself in a circle so I'm facing the shore with the waves lapping against my feet. "Like this?" I yell as a wave crashes over me, filling my mouth with saltwater.

"Yep. Now look over your shoulder, and when you see a wave coming, push yourself off the board and onto your feet, dominant foot back, in a crouch. Just like Ernie and I showed you."

I crane my neck back, pushing up on the board in an imitation of an overweight seal, and I see a wave crashing towards me. Crap. I'm not ready for this. I draw in a deep breath of the salty air and press my hands against the board. Just stand up.

I push against the board and spring to my feet, but my right foot doesn't plant on the board and I go flying off of the board. The wave engulfs me and I tumble under the water, my ankle stinging as the leash keeps the board close to me. I flail my arms and resurface, my hair plastered over my face.

"Riley, are you okay?"

Hands catch on my waist and pull me upright, and I spit a mouthful of saltwater out of my mouth. "Pah--yeah, I'm good."

I rake my hands through my hair to eradicate my resemblance to Cousin It, combing the long dirty blonde strands behind my ears. I blink my stinging eyes and look up at Ross, who still holds my waist with a teasing grin on his face.

"You sure? That was quite a fall."

I shove him away with a grin. "I'm fine--don't need any rescuing here."

"Ready to try again?"

I reach for his arm and pull him back towards me, looking up at him with my best imitation of puppy dog eyes. "I have to try again? Why don't I just watch you and Ernie?" Ross catches my face with his hand, wiping a trail of saltwater from across my cheekbone. "You're not getting away that easy."

I turn towards him so we're chest to chest, body to body, and weave my arms around his shoulders and neck. "Oh really?"

Maybe if I kiss him long enough he'll forget all about surfing and we can go back to the beach and lie in the sun.

He leans toward me, his hot breath leaving a trail of goosebumps on my cold neck. I take his face in my hands, his stubble rough and scratchy beneath my fingertips, and pull him toward me. There's no hesitancy in the way we kiss now--we kiss like we'll never have the chance to again. We kiss like the world might end tomorrow. Ross reaches for me, one hand tangling in my wet, stringy hair and the other taking my chins and angling my face so he can deepen the kiss.

My eyes flutter shut, damp eyelashes cold on my cheeks, and I lean into him, the water rushing and whistling around us as if we're in the midst of our own personal whirlpool. Ross pulls away from me just a little so I can see his eyes inches from mine.

"Hey, you're really pretty," he says, voice an octave lower than normal. He runs his finger along the side of my face and across my cheekbones and nose. "And also kind of hot."

"Just kind of?" I tease. "Rude."

He just laughs at me and the sound is rich and reverberates through my chest. He leans down to kiss me one more time and then pushes me away, gesturing to the abandoned surfboard floating beside us.

"Okay, no more distractions. Go again."

"Dang, you're a drill sergeant, and I would know thanks to Colonel Eugene Olson."

A yell from the beach interrupts us. "Riley, your phone's been ringing incessantly for the last ten minutes. You might want to answer it."

Ross and I both look over and grin at Earnest, forgotten on the beach. "Coming!" I yell, unhooking my leash and tossing it to Ross with a grin. "Have fun!"

I sprint through the waves, nearly falling a few times, and jog towards my discarded shorts where my phone lies. I pick it up and see a few missed calls from Mom. Is something wrong? Ever since they pawned me off on the Covingtons, I've heard hardly anything from either Mom or Dad. I talked to Mom a few weeks ago about my career and going back to school, but got so frustrated that I had to hang up. Maybe Great Aunt Jemima--yes, that's actually her name--finally kicked the bucket and we inherited her fabulous fortune.

"Riley? Is that you?"

Mom's voice is laced with static and I hear her curse their cell phone service provider as if AT&T is personally responsible for the static on the line.

"Yep. What's wrong? Did somebody die?"

"Don't be so vulgar, darling. Everything's fine, but your father and I have pulled some strings at Cornell and we need you to be there this evening for a series of interviews that will allow you to be readmitted to go after--what was it you said you were interested in?"

My jaw drops but I somehow mumble the answer through the haze of confusion. "School psychology."

"Right. If you're serious about this, we can help you get back into Cornell with a generous donation to the new sports complex. But you have to get here by this evening. Your father and I will meet you here."

No. I can't leave. And suddenly the two forces in conflict reach a crux, between my career and Ross. The summer is drawing to a close, and if Cornell does let me in, I might not have a chance to come back to the island before I start school again in the fall.

"But what about the Island--can I come back?"

"I don't know, darling. I thought you didn't even like it? Just pack up your things and get here--that is, if you're serious about this. If not, your father and I will not be providing you with any fiscal support for your career."

An ultimatum. My career, or my summer with Ross. I thought I had more time to end things, more time to reconcile myself to the coming demise of our eager relationship, but not anymore. I have to choose.

I hang up and drop my phone into the sand, turning to find Ross approaching me on the beach.

"Ross, I have something to tell you."

~~~~~

What do you think she's going to do? If she leaves, she might never see Ross again, but if she stays, she misses her chance at getting back into Cornell. What should she do?

Impact Zone

R^{oss}

Impact Zone. (noun). [im-pakt zone]. The location where the waves break.

"Ross, I have something to tell you."

My stomach rolls at the words, and I wonder if this it, if this is the end. Today has been too perfect, too good for a short summer to endure, and the tremor in Riley's voice is the harbinger of news that I'm afraid will break my heart.

Her green eyes are wider than ever, and I glance to her phone, dropped in the sand, and her trembling hands that hang loosely by her side. Even her lower lip shakes and her eyes are glassy with tears.

No. No, this can't be the end. I'm not ready. I'll never be ready.

"Is--is everything okay?" I ask, taking a tenuous step toward her.

Her gaze breaks from mine and she cross her thin arms over her chest. Her glassy eyes scream melancholy, and I want to pull her into my arms and tell her it will all be okay, but what if it won't? What if this is the end?

"No," she murmurs, her chin falling to her chest. "I'm leaving. Tonight--now. I have to go."

I move towards her and take her hands, untangling her arms from her chest, and holding them in mine. "What are you talking about? The summer's not even over yet--you don't have to go anywhere!"

Riley lifts her chin to look at me, her hands icy in mine. I can feel her starting to shake. "I have to go, Ross. It's Cornell. They're going to let me interview for readmittance. I could--I could study clinical psychology, maybe work at a school or...or something. My parents pulled strings and I have to go. I can't risk losing this."

And I know in that moment that I can't ask her to stay even though I want to beg her on my hands and knees to never leave my side. For all my empty talk of summer flings and temporary romance, the churning in my gut tells me that I'm not ready for goodbye. Not yet. Not now. Not ever.

But if Riley has a chance at pursuing her dreams, I can't stop her. I'm going to leave in just over a month anyways, and I know she would never ask me to give up the internship for her. I just--I thought we had time.

My hands drop hers and I pull away. "Now? Tonight?"

She nods, looking at the sand. She kneads her lower lip between her teeth, making it red and swollen and I wish a kiss would make everything go away, but it won't. I've known since the moment we met that this was only for the summer, but...

"Are you coming back?" I ask her, and I let the hope blossom inside of me. I need a chance. I need time to prepare for the inevitable separation.

"I...I don't know," she says, again crossing her arms and turning away from me so she doesn't have to look at me, so I don't have to look at her.

Not yes. Not no. I don't know. She could come back for a final goodbye, but then again, she might not. She might get in her car and drive away and never come back to Long Beach Island. I might never see her again.

"Ry..." I try to finish the sentence, but I can't seem to sort out the words jumbled around in my mind. I like you, love you, want you. Stay. Go. Never leave.

"I don't want to go," she murmurs, and I see the tears rise into her eyes and start to overflow, one dripping down her freckled cheek.

I can't handle the space between us and I reach for her, pulling her into the spot carved into my body just for her. She leans her cheek against my collarbone, her head fitted perfectly beneath my chin, and wraps her arms around my middle.

Don't go, I want to tell her. Maybe if I asked her, she would stay, but this is too good of a chance to pass up--she could return to Cornell, pursuing a degree in something she actually cares about. She'll get great grades because she's a genius, find a perfect job, get married, and have the settled-down life she's always wanted. It's not something I can give her. I'm not even sure that's the future I want, but I know beyond a shadow of a doubt, I don't want to say goodbye.

Riley pulls away from me and I lean towards her, wanting to grab onto her fingers, her hair, her waist, anything that will let me keep her here.

"Will you walk back with me? I only have a few minutes," she says, wiping at her cheeks, red from the brief tears. "Can't keep Colonel Eugene Olson waiting." She smiles up at me through the tears and her attempt at humor, her attempt at making this lighter, only makes everything worse.

"Of course," I say, and I pull my shirt over my head, scarcely knowing what I'm doing. I feel like a robot as I walk beside her, and I try to tell myself that this is real, that the end has finally come.

We can't say anything else as we walk back to the Coventry's house--I wait on the front step of A Pizza the Action while Riley packs her stuff. I pull my knees to my chest and run my hand over my face and through my hair, trying to gather some steely courage I've never had.

I've never been good at goodbyes.

Even when Mom left us, it took me years to finally accept that she was gone. Almost everyone in my life--except for Mom and now Riley--has been a permanent fixture, withstanding the test of time. Sure, the kids and Javier and Earnest and the rest have grown and changed over the years, but they've always been here, just like the peeled boardwalk to the beach and the rickety lifeguard chairs.

But Riley is different. She's quick and temporal and gone before I could really catch ahold of her. And she's about to be gone, maybe for good. If I don't say something, I'm going to lose her, but if I say anything, I might keep her from pursuing her dreams. I'm not perfect, but I won't be so selfish that I hold her back from a career and a future that might make her truly happy.

I have to stay silent even with every word I've ever learned bursting from my lips to try to tell her not to leave.

The door to the pizza shop opens and Riley reappears before I'm ready with only a suitcase, a box, and a half-empty backpack, her meager possessions. She's changed into a straight black dress that shows off her slender frame and long legs and her hair is brushed into a neat ponytail--she looks nothing like the girl who was just surfing and laughing at her every failure. She's transformed before my eyes.

"So this is everything."

"Uh, let me get that for you," I say, taking her suitcase from her and leading the way to her Honda Fit, parked in the corner of the lot.

It takes us only seconds to load the car and she opens the driver's door, preparing to step inside. "I guess this is it," she says with a crooked smile.

No. It can't be.

But I know I have to let her go for her own sake.

"Ry, I..."

She steps closer to me, planting her palm on my chest. "Ross, don't. Don't make this harder than it has to be. This...we were just a summer fling. It was fun...while it lasted."But summer's not over yet.

She refuses to lift her face to look me in the eye and I reach for her, my hands resting at the curve of her waist. She sags toward me, her protesting hand curling into the soft cotton of my shirt. Our foreheads touch and her breath burns hot against my neck.

Don't go.

"Thank you," I whisper.

She tilts her head and looks up at me, her eyes so near that I can trace the gold and blue and brown in the pale green of her eyes. "For what?"

I smile at her softly. "I wouldn't be going on this internship if it weren't for you. Even if...even if we never see each other again..."

"Maybe I'll come back before the end of the summer," she says, her words rushed and short. "You never know."

"Even if you don't, thank you," I say.

These aren't the last words I want to say to her, but they're all I can offer. I want to pull her closer to me and kiss her until we both forget about the impending goodbye, but I don't. I back away, and she's gone from me until we're only connected by our hands, fingers clutching at each other in a final desperate attempt at remembrance.

I stare at where our fingers still latch together, and as much as I tell myself to pull away, to let go, my body no longer obeys my mind.

"Goodbye," Riley says, and she forces the final separation, her pale cold fingers pulling away from mine.

She climbs into the driver's seat and starts the car, backing it out of the parking spot and driving to the turn out. She doesn't wave goodbye. She doesn't look at me in the rearview mirror. She doesn't jump out of the car for one final kiss. She drives away, her tires screeching as she pulls from the parking lot.

And she's gone.

As soon as she's out of sight, I crumble. I fall into a crouch in the parking lot with my head in between my hands, and all the words tumble out.

"Don't go. Please don't go. Stay."

But she can't hear me, and expressing what I'm feeling does nothing but remind me what just drove away. Was I wrong? Should I have told her how I feel? That even though it's only been two months, even though we've only barely met, that I love her despite it all? That I want her to stay here or go to Cornell or travel the world as long as it's with me?

I want to run to the beach and scream all the unsaid words in my head and my heart, everything I've never said to Riley and to Dad and to Mom.

Before Mom died, when we first found out about her disorder, when we learned about the dangers of postpartum psychosis, I should have said my goodbyes. I knew the risks. I knew that we had to keep Mason away from her, that we needed to watch the knives and razor blades and pills. I knew she might do something extreme, but I didn't truly understand what it was like to have someone disappear from my life, leaving only a faded shadow.

I was 19 when she slit her wrists--old enough to remember the blood that seeped beneath the bathroom door. But Ivy, who was two at the time, and Mason, who was only a newborn, don't remember her. They don't remember the trauma, but they also don't remember the vibrant woman she was in her younger days when I was a kid. I remember all of it--the good and the bad, the slow fade into depression and darkness--I remember all of it in perfect detail.

And even though I knew she might make the ultimate choice, I never thought she would. I thought that we were enough, the five of us, to keep her here, but we weren't. I never told her goodbye, and then one day, she ended everything.

Mom never knew what she meant to me because I never told her, just like I didn't say the words I should have said to Riley. Now she's gone, and she doesn't know.

If she ever comes back, I swear I'll tell her how I feel.

~~~~~

Headland

- -

Riley

Headland. Noun. [hed-land]. An area of high elevation more resistant to erosion than surrounding areas and less susceptible to flooding.

I wipe my hands on my black slacks as the admissions counselor speaks, his round glasses perched on the end of his very long witch-like nose. Almost done. Almost done.

"Miss Olson, I believe that between the generosity of your parents," he nods at Mom and Dad, seated behind me with ridiculously wide smiles plastered on their faces. "And your own renewed interest in your education, you are a good candidate for readmittance at Cornell."

Dad even pulled out his Army dress blues for the occasion. "After the stunts you've pulled, we need every vote of sympathy we can get, Riley," Mom told me, referencing Dad's brief bout in Afghanistan. Yes, my family is using my dad's status as an active duty Army colonel to help get me back into college. They know no bounds. At Mr. Ellis's words, Dad's back straightens and he bows his head at the man.

"You have our deepest gratitude, Roger," Dad says. Apparently, when he and Mom went to Cornell back in the olden days, Roger was in the year below them and he acts like my dad is the cat's pajamas, to quote the vernacular.

"Of course," Roger Ellis says, "I'm sure Riley will be a great addition to our school psychology program."

"School psychology," Dad murmurs under his voice, shaking his head as if I'm the biggest disgrace the Olson name has ever seen. Sometimes I really, really wish I had a sibling to take some of the pressure. Of course, with my luck, my fantasy brother or sister would get straight As and go into business and the Army, leaving me as the prodigal child. Maybe I'm better off as is. At least I only have to compete with myself.

"Miss Olson, I understand you've spoken with Dr. Mariani, who will serve as your advisor when you re-enroll in the fall?"

I nod and force myself to speak. "Yeah, I've talked with her a few times. She said that I should be able to finish my degree in a year and a half."

I was so relieved when she told me that. I'm okay with getting the degree I need to go into school psychology, but the prospect of four more years of college made my insides twist into a knot. Luckily, using my previous credits and my semester of study abroad, Dr. Mariani figured out a way for me to finish in only a year and a half. Thank goodness.

"You're very lucky to have reached such an arrangement," Ellis said, tapping his Cornell-emblazoned pen on the mahogany desk. "Especially after dropping out. But I'm sure you'll bring pride to the Olson name."

I puke a little in my mouth as I see Mom and Dad exchange a knowing, amorous look between them. I'm all too aware of their history as Cornell's Cutest Couple of the 90s and Dad's start position on the offensive line of the football team. I'm one hundred percent certain I won't live up to their reputation, and I'm totally fine with that.

"You have, of course, lost your scholarship because of your change in status," Ellis continues. "But I'm sure with your father's eminent career, the tuition will be no problem."

"Oh, she'll have to work!" Dad interrupts in a gruff voice. "We Olsons got to where we are through hard work, and she'll have to learn that lesson. We've been too easy on her over the years."

I think about the eighteen times we moved--soon to be nineteen--and the summer I spent sweating in a pizza shop and sleeping on a bunkbed. Yeah, my life's been real easy. But then an image of Ross comes to my mind unbidden and something pulls inside of me--his dimples, his smile, his voice. I have had it easy compared to Ross. If I have to work in the Cornell dishroom to pay for a year and a half's worth of tuition, I'll do it.

"That's fine. I'll get a job," I say though my nose wrinkles as I imagine scrubbing a toilet in the guys' dorm or picking wet napkins out of cups.

"Well, there are a few work study positions in the counseling office," Roger Ellis says, and my ears perk up. "They're, of course, very competitive and only available for the top students, but maybe..." His voice trails off doubtfully and I almost roll my eyes.

I'll get straight A's for the rest of my life if that means no dishroom duty, and I nod my head up and down with my most innocent smile. "Thank you, Mr. Ellis."

Mom stands up suddenly, straightening the blush pink sheath dress she wore for the occasion. One would think she was the one having the interview. She takes Mr. Ellis's hand and presses it, giving him a warm smile that brings a blush to his face, literally. I didn't get my dad's smarts and reputation or my mom's beauty and charm. Bummer.

"Roger, thank you so much again for making time for our dear little Riley. It's a comfort to know there are still those who value strong family values and patriotism."

Roger looks a little uncomfortable but just nods, smiles, and blushes. "Of course. It's been a pleasure."

Dad gives Roger a salute and he eats that up like he just met the president. Way to play up the whole Army thing, Dad. "Much thanks, Roger."

I rise to my feet, my knees wavering a little, and I curse my weakness. You're in, Ry. Pull it together. But instead, my stomach twists as I remember Ross's voice, rusty from a long day of working on the beach, calling me "Ry." He used to call me Ry. I squeeze my eyes shut--no. I can't think about Ross right now. I can't have a freaking meltdown in the admission counselor's office.

"Riley?" Mom asks, touching the small of my back with her manicured fingers. "Let's go, honey."

She pushes me out the door and I force my legs to obey, shaking my head to get rid of the trance. Don't think about Ross. As if it's somehow possible for my brain to not think about him every moment of the day. Pull it together.

Before I know it, my family unit has made it outside to Dad's SUV, oversized for just him and Mom and still too large with me strapped in the back seat. "What do you say to a celebratory dinner?" Dad says."Steak?"

Of course, Mom and Dad don't care that I would much rather go to Wendy's and have a ten-packet of chicken nuggets with fries and a Frosty. Mom would just sniff and mutter regretfully about how I didn't inherit their superior tastes. I'm not up for a battle, so steak it is. Dad drives to some steakhouse while Mom tries to get him to use the GPS and he protests, saying that he knows where he's going. He doesn't, and we get there 45 minutes later, but the long car ride and the squabbling in the front seat give me time to freak out in the back seat.

I'm going back to Cornell.

I'm going to finish my degree. I'm going to become a school psychologist. I'm going to settle down and be happy. Life will be perfect. Except Ross.

Every thought process ends with that morbid realization. Ross will go abroad and travel the world like he's always wanted and I'll finally find my purpose in life and settle down. Our two paths diverged on a beach in New Jersey. It's over.

But here's the thing--I want it all. I want Cornell and a degree and a white picket fence home. But I also want Ross and his thirst for adventure and the way his lips taste of salty ocean spray. I want him just as much as I want Cornell, and I've spent too much of my time wondering what it is I really want. Now I know, and I can't lose him. I can't forget him. I can't let go of the one thing I know I want.

A shaky sigh escapes my lips as Dad pulls into a parking spot, tense silence filling the SUV. "Let's go," he barks in his Army voice, and we file out of the car in good order.

The dinner is filled with stunted silence and the sound of my dad belching after every single bite of steak like he just can't resist it. I'm glad that no one feels the need to fill the silence with familial conversation because honestly, I can't pretend to be happy right now.

I mean, I am happy. I'm excited about a new career and maybe even a job at the counseling center. That's all well and good, but Ross--it's still raw. It's like a wound that's only been covered with a bandage. It still aches and leaks and demands attention. He hasn't texted me once since I left, and I would be mad, but I think I understand. As much as I want to call him and hear his voice through the phone, I can't bear the pain. I've pulled his name up a thousand times and considered calling, but I couldn't. I couldn't bear it. I couldn't handle hearing his voice and not being able to kiss him or touch him or whisper nonsense in his ear.

And now what happens? He'll leave in just a few weeks, and I start school in a week and a half. I have no reason to go back to the island and he has no reason to come to Cornell. We might never see each other again, and it's not freaking fair. Both Ross and I have just got everything we ever wanted--he gets to travel, I get a purpose. We have everything we ever wanted, but now, something is missing. He's missing.

I've never told anyone I loved them besides my parents, and even then, only when I was a kid. But the words I love you are bitter on my tongue. I know it's crazy, we've only known each other a few months, we're young and stupid, but there's something in my heart--a weight, a heaviness I can't dispel--that says this feeling isn't tampered by youth or inexperience. Whatever is between Ross and I is undeniably real and I'm just going to walk away, let him fade into the rearview mirror, let life steal him from me. Just like I've always let life take everything from me while I sit back and watch it.

Not this time.

I'm done.

I've let life pass me by, cart me around like a freaking passenger, and I'm done. I'm in charge of my life, and I still have a week and a half left before I have to start at Cornell, and I have a car.

I'm going to see Ross.

I stand up from the table and my chair slides back with a squeak. "I'm leaving," I declare, and Mom's face pales and turns red at the same time.

"What are you talking about?" Dad thunders, throwing down his bloodied cloth napkin. "Riley, we put too much into this visit for you to throw it away on a whim!"

Crap. "Oh, no, Dad, I'm coming back when school starts." Dorm life, what a thing to look forward to. "But I'm going back to the island. Just for a few days. I'll be back in plenty of time, and it'll be fine. But I need to go back."

Mom touches my arm, her hand icy. "Riley, just calm down. I know you got rather...attached to your friends there, but you can't just run off. You need to prepare for your semester!"

"I'm an adult," I say, resolution growing with every word. There's time, and Ross deserves more than a half-hearted goodbye. He deserves everything. "I have a care, and I'm going to the island. I swear I'll be back in time, and I'm not wasting this opportunity."

I skedaddle out the door before they can stop me, pulling my phone out to call for an Uber. I consider calling Ross, a smile growing on my face. I'm going to see him again. But no--it's going to be a surprise. I'm going to see him in person, I'm going to tell him how I feel, and I'm going to try to make things work. Somehow.

Two hours later, I'm in my car with a duffle bag packed and Taylor Swift cranked as loud as it goes, and I'm on my way to Long Beach Island.

I'm going to see Ross. I'm going to tell him how I feel, and I swear, if we don't work out, it won't be because I didn't give him everything.

~~~~~

Crest

R oss

Crest. Noun. [krest]. The point on a wave with the maximum value or upward displacement within a cycle.

The promise I made to myself that I would tell Riley how I feel has to come to nothing. She's not here and I'm not about to tell her I love her over voicemail. I love her. The words have ricocheted in my head for the last week since she left. I don't know why I didn't just tell her. I knew--I think I've known for a while now. I shouldn't have let her just leave. I'm a freaking idiot.

Now I only have three weeks before I go to Washington D.C. and from there, to the rest of the world. The internship starts in Honduras, but that's all they've told me so far. I should be more excited than I am, but every time I think about going, I think about Riley. She's the reason I'm finally leaving. She's the reason I have the guts to go after what I want. Except what I want has changed. I want Riley now, too. I love her.

I sigh and lean back against the lifeguard chair, forcing my eyes to refocus on the handful of people still enjoying the very ends of their summer vacations. A chubby toddler in a duck floatie sputters when a wave crashes over him, but other than that, all is quiet on the Long Beach front.

"What's a girl have to do to get rescued by a lifeguard around here?"

I almost fall out of the chair. Riley stands at the foot of the chair in a pair of gym shorts in a tank top, her long hair snapping in the wind as she grins up at me. She's here.

I jump out of the chair into the sand as soon as I see her, falling on one knee and then staggering up again. I don't stop to tell her how happy I am to see her or to tell her I love her. I just pull her into my arms, tight against my chest, and I rest my head in the crook of her neck, breathing in. My hands catch in the material of her tank top and then her hair.

She's here. She came back. She's here.

Her arms hold me as tightly as mine hold her, and I feel her laugh against my shoulder, the sound melodious and sweet. It's been a week, and I've missed her. Gosh, how I've missed her.

"Ry," I whisper into her ear, her hair soft against my face. "You came back."

She reaches for my face and leans her head back to smile at me. "Of course I came back. I couldn't leave you with that lame goodbye, could I? That's hardly--"

But I cut her off. I can't look at her, I can't see her without kissing her. How am I supposed to pretend that the last week didn't almost kill me? That our stunted, brief goodbye in the parking lot wrecked my soul?

Her lips are soft and pliant beneath mine, parting as this kiss says everything I need it to say. I half expect her to pull away or make an excuse like she has before, but not this time. There's a neediness, an eagerness, a desperation in this kiss that heals and breaks my heart at once. My fingers thread in her hair, a hand clutches at the small of her back, and I wonder if two bodies can fuse together so they never have to be apart.

"Ry," I murmur again against her lips.

Her fingernails dig into my shoulders and our lips part, her head resting on my shoulder. "I missed you," she murmurs into my t-shirt.

"I missed you too. How long...how long can you stay?" "I only have a few hours. I'm going back to Cornell, but I needed a real goodbye. You know," Riley leans her head back and grins up at me, her eyelashes dark against her freckled cheeks. "I didn't want you to forget me or anything."

"Never." I run a finger along her cheekbone, memorizing every contour with my eyes and fingers and lips.

"Well, now that's done," Riley says, pulling away from me. "Good bye."

She turns to leave and I laugh at her. "Just wait a second. I'll get Javi to cover for me."

I send Javier a quick text and he shows up on a four wheeler a few minutes later, a smirk on his face. "Hey, Riley. Didn't expect to see you again so soon."

"Take over for me," I tell him, tossing him the key on the lanyard around my neck.

"Your wish is my command." Javier climbs into the lifeguard chair with no other words, and I take Riley's hand.

There's something I have to do.

"Do you have time for one final adventure?" I ask her, my thumb tracing the lines in her palm.

She cocks her head in faux consideration. "I guess so. Where are we going?" I tug on my hand and pull her behind me. "You'll find out."

All I can think is that this is my last chance to tell her how I feel. All I can remember is not having the chance to say goodbye to Mom, to tell her I loved her. As morbid as it is, I need to tell Riley about my mom's death before she can understand just what the words "I love you" mean to me. And I swear she's not leaving before I tell her.

"So, Cornell, huh? You're an Ivy Leaguer again?'

"I know, I know. I sold out," Riley says with a laugh. "But I'm going to have to work for my tuition this time around like the common folk."

"You're practically one of us. I'm finally almost good enough for you." She laughs, but the words ring true. I've never even had a chance with a girl like Riley before. Cultured, intelligent, funny girls who just so happen to be gorgeous and long-legged don't exactly frequent Long Beach Island. And even if they did, they wouldn't be interested in a lifeguard who doubles as a single father to his siblings. Yet here we are. Somehow, she sees me. Somehow, she likes me.

"Oh, don't even joke," she says, leaning against me. "You're a better person than I'll ever be, giving away a year of your life to helping other people. Are you ready?"

"Of course," I say as our feet echo on the sidewalk. "I mean, this is all I've ever wanted. I wouldn't be going if it weren't for you, Ry."

"What? Really?"

"You've pestered me so much about leaving that I figured I finally had to give it a try." Riley laughs. "Look at us, both pursuing our dreams."

"Next thing you know, I'll have two kids, a dog, and a white picket fence," she says.

Next thing you know, some single Ivy League guy will find her and I'll lose my chance. My stomach curdles. What can I ask her, to wait for me? For some indefinite time in the future when I can give her what she deserves? Of course I can't. Should I even tell her how I feel?

But I have to. I can't hold it in. I can't pretend I don't feel it.

"Ross? What are you thinking about?" she asks me, but we're here. The graveyard.

"This is it," I say, gesturing to the cast iron gate in front of the cemetery.

Riley drops my hand and stares at it for a minute. "A cemetery? What the heck?"

"Just bear with me," I say, grabbing her hand and pulling her inside.

Mom's lot is in the far corner of the cemetery underneath the shade of a poplar tree. This spring, Ivy and I planted five different kinds of flowers around her tombstone to signify the five family members she left behind, and the flowers have sprouted all around the stone, nearly blocking out her name. It's what she would have wanted. I wonder if Dad knows who planted them when he visits every day.

I tug on Riley's hand and take her to the foot of the stone. "This is--my mom died. I know I never really told you what happened to her, but she died five years ago after Mason was born."

Riley reads the gravestone and then studies me, all the humor gone from her eyes. "Ella Montgomery," she whispers.

It's the first time I've heard Mom's name out loud in years and it cracks something inside of me. "She--she killed herself," I spit out, the words still bitter and pungent on my tongue. "She had postpartum depression that lead to psychosis after Mason, and then, she--" Riley stops me with a hand on my arm, her eyes welling with tears I've never seen before. Her forehead rests on my arm for a moment. "Ross, I'm so sorry."

A lump rises in my throat but I swallow it. I'm not here to cry over my mother; I'm here to show Riley why this is so important to me. "Thanks. But I--I know this is weird, but I had to show you this. I had to tell you."

"Why?"

"I never got to say goodbye," I murmur, my eyes fastened on the daisies blossoming at the foot of the stone. "I never got to tell her I love her, and I'll regret that for the rest of my life."

Riley's breath stops and she stares up at me. There's something different in her gaze. Something has changed in the way she looks at me. I don't see the fear and cynicism; there's only aching vulnerability.

I take her hands into mine and turn them palm up, tracing every line. How can I say this so she understands how important these words are to me? But maybe she knows. Maybe she knows that I don't say things lightly after Mom. Maybe she understands that I wouldn't say this unless I was absolutely certain. And I am. I've never felt this way before, like my soul is wrapped up in someone else's. It's terrifying and mystifying and enthralling.

"Ry, I don't know how to say this," I whisper, finally raising my eyes to hers. Her eyes are glassy with tears--from sorrow or hope or heartbreak, I can't tell. I'm feeling all three.

"I love you."

The words come from her mouth before I can articulate them and my jaw drops. Riley, the girl terrified of commitment and vulnerability and maybe even me, just told me the words I can barely hold in.

"Are you serious?" I ask her, my words stuttering.

"That's what you were gonna say, right?" she asks, her cheeks blushing pink. "If not, then I take it back."

"Yeah, I...I love you," I finally stutter, starting to laugh. "I had to tell you. I didn't think you'd say it--I didn't think you felt the same way, but I had to tell you."

She steps closer to me until our breath mingles. "Yeah, well, I didn't really know I felt this way until I walked out on parents and drove a billion hours to come here to say goodbye. Again."

I touch her chin and tilt it up, the smile on my face unstoppable. "So you love me, huh?" "Don't make me say it again," she whispers, rising onto her tiptoes to kiss me.

I kiss her back, bending so we become one. She loves me. I never imagined this, that these feelings were mutual. One summer, and I'm lost.

"I love you, Ross Montgomery," she whispers in my ear as she kisses my jaw.

"I love you too," I murmur back.

The words I've held in for so long I now can't contain. I love her. And I want to beg her to stay but I can't.

Hours pass in a haze of newfound love and overt attraction under the lamplight of the boardwalk, but everything is tainted. Life isn't all sunshine and rainbows. Riley has to go back to Cornell and I'm going to travel the world. For at least nine months, I won't see her. I can't ask her to wait for me, but I want her to. I can't promise her we'll work out because I might never even see her again. Love has to be enough.

The hours pass too quickly and leave us standing in front of Riley's car. The hourglass has run out of sand. The magic dress is fading. Summer is over

Riley leans back against her car and inspects her fingernails. "So what happens now?"

I lean my head back and study the stars as if they can give me the answer I need. "I can't ask you to wait."

"You don't have to."

"It'll be nine months, Ry. No cell phone coverage. A lot can change."

She could fall in love. I could get attacked by a band of monkeys. Who knows.

"Do you...do you think we'll change?" she asks, her voice trembling.

I finally look at her and step closer, boxing her in with my hands on either side of her head. "No, but I won't hold you back, Ry."

"Give me your phone," she says, reaching around me to fish it out of my back pocket. "Send me a letter or a postcard or something. If, you know, you want to."

"I want to."

She smiles as she types her address into my phone. "Good."

The moment for goodbye comes and passes and neither of us does or says anything. What can we say when neither of us wants to leave? What happens between us now? This summer on the island brought us together, but it's fleeting and nearly over.

That's when an idea hits me.

"I have a proposition."

Her face blanches. "If you propose, I swear—"

"Not that kind of proposition." I laugh at her shocked expression. "Next summer, I'll be here again. If you still feel the same way you do now, meet me here." Riley opens her mouth to say something, but I stop her with a finger to her lips. "Don't promise me now, Ry. A lot can change. But if...if we still love each other a year from now, meet me here."

She nods solemnly, eyes glassy. I study her for a long moment, her pale skin and freckles and round green eyes. I miss her even though she's still here.

I lean forward and kiss her, our bodies melding against her car as her arms twine around my neck. I kiss her to sear her memory into my brain so when I start to forget, I can bring this to mind and remember what I'm coming home for.

The kiss ends too soon, but I know the end is already past us. We can't live on borrowed summer time any longer.

"So I guess you won't forget me, huh?" Riley asks with a smirk at the corner of her lips.

"I love you, Ry. I promise."

She chews on her lip and touches my face, searching it.

"I love you too."

But will it be enough? Only time and next summer will tell.

Rift Valley

R iley & Ross

Rift valley. Noun. [rift val-ee]. A deep valley that forms where two plates move apart.

~~~~~

Dear Ross,

Hey, remember me? Duh, of course you do. Who could forget. It's the weekend before finals here at Cornell and I'm procrastinating by talking to you. Don't you feel important? It's weird--even when I'm trying to memorize Piaget's stages of cognitive development, you still come into my mind. I wish we'd taken more pictures this summer. I just have one crappy selfie with saltwater on the screen hung behind my desk. It doesn't feel like enough to sum up one entire summer. But then again, sometimes summer feels like a dream.

I guess I should tell you about my fascinating life. It's cold and snowy here, and all I want to do is hide under a blanket with fluffy socks and Parks and Rec. If you were here, I bet you'd say we should go sledding or build a snowman or something, but I'm too boring for that kind of thing. School is good, by the way. My roommate, I told you about her in my last letter, is actually pretty cool. We're not best friends or anything, but I don't want to shank her in the night, so I guess that's a bonus. Plus, I'm going to live off-campus starting next semester to save money on room and board. And I'm going to cook for myself, so this may be the last letter you ever receive because I'm either going to poison myself or starve myself.

Oh, and I got a new job for next semester! I think I told you I got stuck vacuuming this year--still better than the dish room--but if I get a GPA about 3.75 in my Psych classes, then my advisor said I can work at the counseling center. I'm really excited because this could lead to career opportunities--I just said career opportunities without laughing. I'm really growing up.

Christmas is going to be awful. Mom and Dad are taking me with them to D.C. for some Christmas ball thing and they've insisted I can't just stay home in previously mentioned comfy socks. No, I have to go, and they even bought me this bedazzled dress. You'd compliment me if you were here, and then die laughing because there are gems and glitter literally everywhere. Plus, my parents have appointed themselves my matchmakers. I think they're worried I'll run off and fall in love with some lifeguard--ridiculous, right? They're trying to get this stuffy Harvard guy who wears coral shorts in all his Facebook pictures to go to the ball as my date. Don't worry, I'm not interested. He's more of a sailor than a lifeguard, and I need to keep a lifeguard around what with the last time I went swimming.

I don't have anything else to tell you. I know you're feeding starving kids in Africa or whatever, but write me a letter sometime soon. I miss you, and summer is too far away.

Love,

Riley

~~~~~

Dear Riley,

I miss you like crazy. Last night I dreamed you were here in my arms, and waking up completely sucked. I want to be kissing you right now, not stretching my muscles that are sore from ditch digging.

Can it be summer now?

I'm mostly kidding. As much as I miss you, this year has been awesome so far. I spent Christmas in Latvia and had gingerbread and bacon rolls--yes, bacon rolls--after seeing the world's first Christmas tree. It was incredible. Now I'm in Kenya digging ditches for some new water pipes. My arms and shoulders ache from using muscles I didn't even know I have--me, the lifeguard and professional box picker upper. Most of their tools are really old and broken which just makes the work take longer, but still, it's exciting. We're working together to finish the water pipe and next week, they'll be able to run water from a well three miles away to houses all throughout the village. It's cool.

I got an actual letter from Dad this week, believe it or not. He's stuck with the grief counseling and he said he was thinking about going to Alcoholics Anonymous. His words, not mine. He sent me notes from Ivy, Mason, and Sammy. I miss them almost as much as I miss you. As much as I love traveling and everything, I don't think I want to travel for the rest of my life. Maybe just once a year, in the summer maybe? I'll have to look for a good traveling partner.

Did Lucy tell you that they're getting married? Ernie sent me a wedding invitation and asked me to be a groomsman. Apparently they're getting married on the beach this summer. Man, I feel too young to have friends who are getting married, but Ernie and Lucy, I think they'll make it work. By the way, are you going to be busy on the weekend of July 8th? I might need a plus one.

I still have four and a half more months of this internship. I mean, that's partially a good thing. I've seen things I never even imagined, Ry. I thought I would care more about nature and scenery and stuff, but it's the people that amaze me most. There's so much resilience and strength in people--I think I kind of gave up on people after Mom committed suicide and Dad lost himself. But there are good people out there, Ry. Don't worry though, you're still the best.

I don't have anything else to say but I really don't want to end this letter because it's my only connection to you. The next time I travel the world, I'm just getting an international cell phone plan. Writing letters is not as romantic as I thought it'd be.

For now, I love you and I miss you and I'll see you soon. Meet you on the first day of summer?

Ross

Tidal Wave

R^{oss}

Tidal Wave. Noun. [tahyd-l weiv]. A widespread or over-whelming manifestation of an emotion or phenomenon.

It's the first day of summer, and she's not here.

Riley didn't come.

I was sure she'd show up in her crappy car with her hair all wind-blown from having the windows down, a smile on her face and her freckles glowing in the sun. I figured she'd hop out, smile at me, and tell some stupid joke in the time it took me to run to her, kiss her, hold her.

But she's not here.

Javier keeps telling me there are still a few more hours in the day--it's only nine o'clock, and she might still show up. I guess it's possible, but the part of me that knew she would come has died. Hope has died.

I know it's been almost a year since we've seen each other, but we've exchanged some letters and I thought things are the same, or they would be when she came back. I still love her, more than I did when I left. Absence makes the heart grow fonder or some crap like that. I finished my internship and now I just want her. I'll move wherever she is. I'll marry her as soon as she'll let me. In all the places I went and the people I saw, nothing compared to her.

That's what I wanted to tell her today--that nothing compares to her. That of everything I want, I want her most of all. That I'll give up anything to spend more time with her. But she's not here.

Maybe what we had was only meant for one summer--a magic that only lasted while the sun was high in the sky. Maybe it faded for her as time passed and she forgot us, or worse yet, she remembered and moved on. Maybe I've clung to someone who hasn't clung to me.

"Man, Ross. You look like someone ran over your puppy."

I glare at Javier. "You ran over my puppy, or Ivy's puppy, two summers ago."

Javier shrugs and sits in the sand next to me a few yards from the giant bonfire in the middle of the beach. "Let it go, man."

"She didn't come."

"Give her a little more credit. Maybe she's running late."

"She's not coming, Javi." I lean back and rest my head on my hands, the sand cool beneath me. "I really thought she would. I was sure of it."

Javier sighs and cranes his neck back, eyes on the stars. "She was crazy about you, Ross. Didn't she tell you she loved you? That doesn't just go away."

I rub my forehead, pain searing through my skull from a long week of loading boxes and my first day back in the lifeguarding stand. Does love just go away like that? Do the feelings fade when you're so far apart? I don't know. In all honesty, I have no idea what I'm doing, but I thought that what Riley and I had would last the year apart. Maybe I'm just some delusional hopeless romantic.

I close my eyes to block out the stampeding thoughts. Riley didn't come, but tomorrow's going to be another day just like this one. I'll have to get up and move on and pretend everything's fine. Maybe it will be, maybe it won't.

My thoughts blur and exhaustion takes over, relieving me from the aching reality of the present.

"Hey, it's my favorite hot lifeguard. I thought you'd be a little more excited to see me."

The voice breaks through the grogginess in my brain and I rub at my eyes and find sand on my hands and face. I know that voice. I sit up, leaning back on my hands, as I regain my bearings. The beach. The first day of summer. Riley.

Riley.

I open my eyes, the night dark around me and the once booming bonfire now a dying flicker. And I see her. She's sitting next to me on the sand, her arms wrapped around her perfect legs and her head tilted as she smiles at me.

"It's about time, sleepyhead."

"Ry...you're here."

My tongue is thick in my mouth. There's so much more I want to say, but I can't. I'm awestruck. The wind blows her long auburn hair over her eyes, shining, round, green. Hope surges in my chest. She came. She's here.

"Well? Are you going to say anything?" she says, tucking the flyaway strand between her hair.

I look around--I must have fallen asleep and the rest of the islanders returned home. It's just me and the campfire and Riley. She's here.

I turn towards her, my eyes hungrily consuming every square inch of her, from her freckled forehead to her flip-flopped feet. She's perfect. I look at her hand in the sand and reach for it and my fingers tremble as I touch hers. After a year of remembering her through faded pictures and frayed memories, she's now here in full color and my heart hammers in my chest.

"Riley," I murmur, lifting her hand from the sand and kissing the back of her knuckles. Goosebumps break out over her skin.

"What, didn't think I'd show?" she teases, touching my face and resting her hand on the curve of my jaw. Shock and electricity tingle through me at the touch, long desired but also long absent.

"You...you were late," I stutter, my brain still catching up to my body.

"I had a meeting, but I drove all through the night. I'm sorry," she says, the joking gone from her voice. I look from her hand to her eyes and find the wide eyes glassy and brimming with tears.

"Riley," I murmur again, moving towards her. I reach for her and tuck my hand around the back of her head, pulling her lips to mine.

Kissing her is better than I remembered. This moment washes away the nine month absence and the sparse letters and desperate longing. Her mouth is hot and burning on mine, and I lean into her as she arches into me. My hands come to rest on either side of her as she falls back into the sand, her hands in my hair and mine at the curve of her waist.

Our bodies tangle and collide, breath hot and heavy and hands explorative and venturing. Nine months of longing wash through our sandy kisses and fervent whispers. Finally, Riley's hand catches in the throat of my henley and she pushes me back, a blush on her cheeks and a smile on her lips. I lean back onto my knees and she crosses her legs, grinning at me.

"Hey, slow down. We have lots of time for that."

"Do we?" I whisper.

"All the time in the world. I hear there's a pizza shop hiring?" Riley says, that familiar teasing light in her eyes.

I sit back on my knees and study her for a long luxurious moment, the dying bonfire casting shadows on her freckled face. The words I've been longing to say pour out of me.

"Ry, I still love you," I say, taking her hands in mine. "More than I did when you left, and I'll love you more tomorrow than I do right now." I look down at her hands and chuckle. "Even though that doesn't really seem possible right now."

Riley pulls one hand from my grasp and turns her face away as she tucks hair behind her ears. "Things didn't--they didn't change?"

"No. I mean, they did. I saw the world. I grew up. I helped others instead of just myself. But Ry, you didn't fade even after months without you. I realized how much better you are--how you stand out among everything I've seen in the entire world. I still love you, Ry. It was more than a summer--we're eternal. Forever."

The words rush out of me in a torrent, tangled and stuttered, but they emerge. Riley stares at me as I speak, and I can't read her expression, but I realize it doesn't matter. She's here, so she still cares, and even if she doesn't love me, at least I could tell her everything.

"So I take it you missed me?" A smile quirks at her lips and I have to resist the urge to lean in and kiss her. We have lots of time for that.

"Yeah, I guess so. Did I forget to mention that?"

She laughs and shoves me in the chest and I fall backwards into the sand, our laughter mingling in the night air and rising to the stars above us. She falls on my chest and then scooches into the sand next to me. I lay my arm across the sand and she rests her head against it, curving into me.

"So?" I ask, looking at her and the long eyelashes fluttering against her cheeks.

"So? I still love you too, you idiot."

She leans her head back and kisses me again, slow and deep and long this time.

Riley and I aren't just summer passion and stolen kisses and playful adventures. Our love is deep and long and eternal. When we first met, it was me that rescued her from the waves, but I had no idea that our roles would soon reserve. Riley saved me from my mundane life and squandered dreams and enabled me to live again. She's given me a new life that I only want to spend with her.

"I love you," she whispers and I grin against her lips as she kisses me again.

"I love you too."